Storm Constantine's Wraeththu Mythos

WHISPERS OF THE WORLD THAT WAS

Storm Constantine's Wraeththu Mythos

WHISPERS OF THE
WORLD THAT WAS

E. S. Wynn

IMMANION
PRESS

Stafford, England

Storm Constantine's Wraeththu Mythos:
Whispers of the World That Was
By E. S. Wynn
copyright © 2015 Storm Constantine, E S Wynn

Cover Art: Ruby
Wraeththu Mythos Logo: Ruby
Map of Megalithica by Andy Bigwood
Editor and Interior Layout: Storm Constantine

Set in Palatino Linotype

IP0043

ISBN 978-1-907737-66-4

An Immanion Press Edition
http://www.immanion-press.com
info@immanion-press.com

THE HISTORY OF WRAETHTHU
A NEWCOMER'S GUIDE

Storm Constantine

The novels set within the Wraeththu Mythos are published with the intention that they be accessible to everyone, whether or not they have read all of the preceding books and stories. This introduction is provided to give readers new to the Mythos an overview of the Wraeththu world and how it's evolved, and I hope it will also be of interest to long-standing fans.

The Wraeththu Mythos stories first appeared in print in 1987, with the publication of 'The Enchantments of Flesh and Spirit', which was the initial volume in the trilogy 'The Wraeththu Chronicles', but I'd written stories about these beings since I was a teenager. The book – when published – was described as 'ground breaking' because of some of genre taboos it challenged. 'Enchantments' was followed by the final two installments of the trilogy: 'The Bewitchments of Love and Hate' (1988) and 'The Fulfilments of Fate and Desire' (1989). The books were published by Macdonald in the UK and TOR Books in America.

From the very start, something within Wraeththu – perhaps my own love of that world and its inhabitants – captured the hearts of many fans, who remained loyal to it, even when for over fifteen years I didn't write any new Wraeththu stories. Fans kept it alive through fan fiction – creating their own stories set within the Mythos.

I realized I'd entered new territory for genre fiction with Wraeththu – a race that sprang from the ruins of human civilization after humanity had all but destroyed their own environment. Were Wraeththu the world's revenge on its savage, selfish children, or were they perhaps the outcome of a scientific experiment, designed to save the human race, that went wrong? The aspect that most set the book apart from what it might sit beside on book store shelves was that Wraeththu are androgynous – having both male and female physical aspects. While androgynes, or hermaphrodites, had been seen in science fiction and – more rarely – fantasy before, they had never been explored in such a way as I sought to explore them. Hara – as Wraeththu are known – are magical, and more powerful in many respects than humans, whilst also being deceptively waiflike in some cases. Warriors and sorcerers, farmers and diplomats; familiar roles perhaps, but robed in very different forms. Wraeththu sexuality is a source of power, an ability to transcend mundane reality as well as being an extremely spiritual practice.

When the books first appeared, eyebrows were raised, along with criticisms among reviewers, some of whom weren't sure what to make of the explicit and uncompromising exploration of sex between Wraeththu – known as aruna within the books. In those days, sex, relationships and deep characterization were not often a feature of genre fiction. Also, the relationships in the Wraeththu world perhaps seemed even more intimate and unsettling because I chose to write the trilogy from a first person viewpoint – albeit through the eyes and mouths of different characters for each book. This, I felt, brought more immediacy to the narrative, and also drew the reader in far closer, but again – from my own reading within the genres of science fiction and fantasy – it didn't appear to be a common viewpoint to use in genre fiction at the time. That said, writers who greatly inspired me – Tanith Lee and Jane Gaskell to name but two – *did* use this viewpoint wonderfully and that obviously encouraged me to experiment with it myself.

Another problem for some critics was my use of pronouns, which often gave rise to misconceptions about the work. I elected to use the pronoun 'he' to describe hara. At the time, when I faced this labeling quandary, the male pronoun seemed less gender specific than the female version. Using "it" was out of the question, and while I played with new pronouns such as "ey" and "eir", these felt clunky to me and interfered with the flow of the story. Also, because of how hara initially came into being, the use of the masculine pronoun was more appropriate. More of that in a moment.

Some readers simply could not get past the pronoun and predictable prejudices came into play, from both hard line feminists and bigoted homophobics, who could only see hara as a form of gay man. Feminists particularly objected to the fact that only human males could become hara. The term inception describes the transfusion of blood between har and human, and the subsequent mutation. How could it be fair (or even, gods forbid, politically correct) for only men to survive? Again, critics missed the point: hara were initially men *stranded* in a world without women, in which they had to become half female themselves. This book you have in your hands delves deeper into this horror story for men!

Later in the first trilogy, I did introduce the Kamagrian, who were rare 'incepted' women or were born to hara as something different to a standard har – even within the world of Wraeththu there is variance, and 'normality' within individuals is not and cannot be clearly defined. Gender is fluid.

Still, the knee jerk reactions to Wraeththu illustrated uncompromisingly that I could offend people at either extreme of the political spectrum. And that was before the spiritual aspect was considered with its distinctive pagan flavor. (Back in the 80s, you still had to be careful with being open about being a 'witch'.) So taboos were cracking and smashing in every direction.

Another difficulty was that the word hermaphrodite had fallen into disfavor. It was regarded as disrespectful to people displaying characteristics of both genders, who should be described as being 'intersex'. (This has happened with other words when they were applied somewhat carelessly to minority groups, such as Mongol for those with Downs Syndrome.) Personally, I felt the word hermaphrodite should be reclaimed, as it is not in any way insulting in its original sense. It derives from Greek mythology, from the story of Hermaphroditus, who was the son of the god Hermes and the goddess Aphrodite. Hermaphroditus was a handsome youth, who rejected the amorous advances of the water nymph Salmacis. The nymph came across Hermaphroditus while he was bathing and threw herself onto him, begging the gods that they should never be parted. The gods, partial to taking all mortal entreaties literally, transformed the pair into a single androgynous being. In later times, this term was then used to describe any human born with ambiguous sexual characteristics, or who displayed aspects of both genders. But the word hermaphrodite was seen as politically incorrect, and the cold, scientific term intersex must be used instead. To me, Hermaphroditus, far from being the embodiment of a medical condition, pinned down beneath harsh clinical light, personifies instead magic and love, as well as the swiftness and beauty of nature, and its unpredictable and shifting faces. Humans and animals appear in myriad different forms and variances; who has the right to say what is 'normal'? I didn't in the 80s – and don't now – see hermaphrodite as a derogatory term, and feel that androgynes in our world should reclaim it, as pagans successfully reclaimed the word 'witch'.

Still, people's prejudices aside, Wraeththu's fandom continued to grow and thrive. I returned to writing within the Mythos with the publication of *'The Wraiths of Will and Pleasure'* in 2003, the first of *'The Wraeththu Histories'*, (followed by *'The Shades of Time and Memory'* (2004) and *'The Ghosts of Blood and Innocence'* (2005)). In 2003, I also started up Immanion Press to publish my back catalogue and – as it turned out – the new Wraeththu trilogy in the UK. TOR books took the series for publication in the States. At the same time, having been introduced to fan fiction and finding some of it well written, I wanted to give something back to the people who'd kept Wraeththu alive and well while I'd been away from their world. I offered to publish the best of the Wraeththu fan fiction writers, both through novels and short stories. Any submissions we received would be elevated above fan fiction to become 'shared world', which is seen as more 'respectable'.

The first Wraeththu shared world novel was *'Breeding Discontent'*, by Wendy Darling and Bridgette Parker (Immanion Press 2003). To coincide with the inauguration of Immanion Press, the publication of my new novel, and the Mythos story by Bridgette and Wendy, a convention for Wraeththu fans was held in England – Grissecon. This convention was so successful that my colleagues at Immanion Press and I went on to run similar program streams at Dragon*Con in Atlanta, Lunacon in New York and Feencon in Bonn.

I've since written three more Wraeththu novels – the Alba Sulh sequence, which includes *'The Hienama'*, (2005) *'Student of Kyme'* (2008) and *'The Moonshawl'* (2014). Other Mythos novels by different writers include *'Terzah's Sons'* by Victoria Copus (2005) and *'Song of the Sulh'* by Maria J Leel (2012), as well as a series of short story anthologies edited by Wendy Darling and myself. All of these titles are available through Immanion Press as printed books and also in ebook format.

'Whispers of the World That Was' is the latest Wraeththu Mythos novel and brings a completely new vision to the world of hara. Writers always work with 'what ifs?' In E. S. Wynn's case, this was: what if incepted hara could not accept their new state of being and tried to deny it? What if such hara existed within a landscape that had for some time been isolated and estranged from humanity even before humans lost their hold on the world? What if...?

Well, the story is here to discover. E. S. Wynn – whose work has already appeared in two of the Wraeththu Mythos anthologies – brings a fresh new voice to the world of hara. This is a voyage of discovery – for the characters and readers alike.

CHAPTER 1

First dive of the day.

The water in the sea of the Valley-That-Was is cool, a nice contrast to the warm summer air blowing in from The Rift. It's a little murky beneath the surface, but with the plastic-wrapped flashlight and my goggles, I can see far enough ahead to catch the glint of light on the shards in the windows of rows upon rows of sunken towers. It's peaceful beneath the waves, amidst the ruins of humanity. Fish gather in flickering, glittering schools, cruise silted streets like metallic birds, barely disturb the dirt, the mud that covers cars, trucks, buses.

Ahead of me, another light shifts, sends a beam to the bottom. *Stoff.* The closest thing I have to a best friend, Stoff is one of my diving partners, one of the crew members who calls Captain Hima's salvage trawler home. Besides the two of us and Hima, there's Davy, Ray and Yuri. Ray usually stays topside with Hima, watches the readings on finicky equipment, brings us any tools we might need, but don't have on us. Yuri's good with locks, and he's small, good at sliding through spots too narrow for Davy, Stoff and I.

In the silence, Yuri's light rises, does a quick figure-eight. Stoff stops, and as I look, I see Yuri point, indicate something in the mud below. *Good eyes.* I push deeper into the sea, reach out, spread my fingers through silken silt as I touch bottom, dig, find the cool smoothness of metal. *Government generator,* I realize. I glance back, catch Stoff's eyes, then Yuri's, give him a thumb's up. *Really good eyes.*

Each dive lasts a little under an hour, but we make between four and six dives every day in the warm season. Throughout the week, we gather what we can, what we know there's a market for back in Cinder Hill, and then on Saturdays we pack it into pickup trucks on the shore of a saltwater marsh east of the ruins of Stock Town, drive it inland for the Sunday market.

Government generators are great salvage. There are always buyers in Cinder Hill willing to pay top dollar for generators whether they work or not, government generators especially. Gov-gennys have a reputation for being tough, for being easy to fix, easy to clean, with lots of redundancy built in. Occasionally we find one that only needs a quick tune-up, but these days, after years of sitting at the bottom of the sea in the Valley-That-Was, most of the gennys we winch up are just a lot of metal with a lot of potential.

Davy hits the radio he carries in a plastic satchel. Five blips on the button is code for *winch*. The hook hits the water a moment later, sinks. Yuri meets it half way, then guides it down to the mud. I back off a little, give him room, let him do the honors.

Government generators are rare, but there are plenty of other relics of humanity's reign on Earth to fish out of the muck. Spare parts always sell well. Computer components, canned goods, liquor– the Valley-That-Was is a gold mine, but few people have the patience, the equipment or the interest to dive forty, fifty, a hundred feet just to pick the crumbs out of the trash. Even Stoff and I take a break from it in the winter time, save our cash and hole up in his cabin in the foothills east of Cinder Hill until the first heat wave comes. Last year, I rebuilt a bike in the off-season, figured out how to get an old VCR/TV combo unit to play tapes with power from a highway solar cell and a deep cycle battery. Brought back memories, memories of the way things were.

The way things were before.

The Rift. The Rift of the Damned. That's what they call what's left of the western coast of Megalithica now. Used to be coast, mountains east of that, a central valley full of cities and farms, then more mountains as you got closer to the state line. Used to be lots of open land, lots of skyscrapers and long, winding highways. Not anymore. Nowadays, most of the skyscrapers are at the bottom of the sea of the Valley-That-Was, or they're out to the south, buried in ash, lava-rock, drowned in the boiling water off the coast there. There's more ocean than asphalt out here now, which is fine by me. Even when I was human, I didn't care much for the cities. Cinder Hill, the sleepy, backward little burg I grew up in– it's changed too, but at least it's still above the waves.

I've lived in The Rift off and on my whole life. Only when the fabric of civilization started to unravel and everything began to fall apart did me and a girlfriend pack everything we had in a rental trailer, hitch it to the back of a truck and make our way north to Duwamish. Well, the city that would become Duwamish. Seemed like a good idea at the time. Seemed like a chance for a new start, for a new beginning in a place where the money came easier and bellies were just a little fuller. Wasn't long after that the rich either fled or evacuated the hills, came down into the cities of the Valley-That-Was with some idea of finding safety in numbers. The rural towns, the gold country, everything closer to the mountains was left to the poor, the indigent, the people that the Government didn't think were worth saving.

Funny how things work out. Even after the girlfriend and I split, I felt lucky, felt like I'd gotten ahead of the curve by moving up to Duwamish. Sure, parts of the city were turning to shit quick, but the people back home had worse problems. Overcrowding in the cities, starvation and drought in the rural and agrarian areas. The Government did what it could, filled the streets of the cities with emergency supplies, practically dropped a generator on every corner of the state capital to keep power flowing. I remember catching the updates on the news, watching footage of smoky roads, of refugees in dust masks dragging grimy suitcases, of crowds crammed into towers and office buildings that had been sitting vacant for years, abandoned after the credit crunch and the following economic collapse. Disease, diverted food trucks, people begging and bleeding in the street, nervous and exhausted rent-a-cops amped up on god-knows-what snapping suddenly, killing innocents – it was a mess.

Then the floodwaters came. The ocean rose and drowned everything, washed away all the trash, human or otherwise, in a sudden, cleansing tide.

I caught that on the news too. By then, cable and internet service were spotty, so I was watching the world fall apart on the beat up old CRT hanging in the back of a coffee shop on Roosevelt Way instead of looking for work I knew I'd never find. October the 25th. That's when the volcanoes finally broke the bay, rose like fiery fingers from the depths of the boiling waters. Six of them in all – six peaks spread across the waves from Bodega to Baja, and all of them spewing, belching smoke, shaking the coast until it cracked apart, dumped twenty million people into the rising sea.

The worst part about it wasn't the deaths, though. So many of those people in the cities were already dead, were just days away from eating each other alive. The real tragedy was the fact that the cracking of the coast didn't happen all at once. The volcanoes, the flooding – with something like that, there's always warning. Most of the millions crammed into the southern and coastal metropolises stuck through the earthquakes that came as the most obvious warning signs, but the worse things got, the more people broke from the masses and tried to move inland, tried to move north. The lands that would become The Rift and the Valley-That-Was were all but lawless then, packed with gangs. Even if you could get out of a given city, chances were you'd be robbed, raped and killed on the road.

Even still, the cities on dry land were quickly swamped with starving refugees. The Government had overextended itself in the cities that had sunken into The Rift, and with storms flooding, ripping into Megalithica's eastern coast, what was left of the relief forces pulled out of the west, left it to private security, to the refugees, the poor, the unfortunate.

To us.

I wasn't har in those days, but when the Federal Government turned their back on the west, I think everyone realized it was only a matter of time before the gangs took control of our cities, our towns, what was left of our civilization. I didn't wait to see how it would turn out in the north. I left Duwamish just before Manticker slaughtered his famous seventy, though I only heard about it months later. Months after I was incepted, months after a har covered in tattoos told me I was no longer human, that I was now *Uigenna*, one with the tribe that had risen to claim the lands of Megalithica's northwest.

I try not think much about how I became har. None of us who crew Captain Hima's trawler do. We all have different stories about how it happened, but they all end the same. Myself, I was taking a piss at a highway rest stop when a gang of Uigenna punks caught me, dragged me to some dark, greasy garage and cut my arms open with a pair of shining switchblades. I remember the way the blood they filled me with changed me, how much it *burned*, how, when it was all over, one of those sons of bitches bent me across a table and tried to make me enjoy whatever it is we do with our genitals now. I put up with it until I got my hands on my bike again, and then I was gone. Didn't look back. Didn't have any second thoughts. I haven't seen any of those hara since.

The Rift of the Damned. The sea of the Valley-That-Was. It was a long, hard ride back to Cinder Hill, back to the town I'd grown up in. Gangs that caught me on the broken road, stopped me – some of them were friendly, offered me food, companionship, called me *brother*, but not all of them were so generous. Others held me at gunpoint or knifepoint, demanded I come with them to this town or that city. In the end, I always managed to get away, usually with my hide intact, but not always. I still have scars, nasty scars, deep in the skin from some of my "brothers" among the Uigenna who had other plans for me than the return to Cinder Hill I had in mind.

Davy hits the radio again, five times, and the winch goes tight. The steel cable pulls taut, brings me back. Yuri slides along the side of the genny like a snake, frees it from a cluster of heavy, rubbery cords as it rises from the mud. The rest of us back off, watch the silt bloom around the boxy, scarlet treasure. The flag stamped on the side stirs memories in me, memories of days spent in classrooms, of stuffy clothes, of standing with my hand over my heart, my lips whispering a prayer for an empire that was dead long before the Wraeththu came and finished it off.

Stoff glances over at me and I meet his eyes. Of the forty-nine hundred and some-odd people who once called Cinder Hill home, only a handful remained when I pulled into town, and none of them were folks I knew. Stoff was one of the first hara I met when I arrived, but he, like so many others in Cinder Hill, was a transplant from somewhere else, some place in the Valley-That-Was. Cinder Hill itself slid back to something like its gold rush, wild western roots and became again a sort of trade hub for folks living in homes and on ranches further up in the hills and the woods, so by the time I pulled into town, there was plenty of activity and plenty of work to go around with guys still clinging to the way things were, the way they used to be. Good folks, hill folks, sons of farmers and miners and refugees from the dust bowl who all wanted to grow up to be cowboys, bikers or greasy, beefy mechanics. People like me who were more interested in hanging on to what was left of our dusty humanity instead of falling over into the ways of the weird world that always seemed to be creeping in from the sides all around us. I suppose at first it was nostalgia that kept me there, but working odd jobs with Stoff also gave me purpose, gave me something to do, gave me a reason to stay through the cold season. Wasn't long until Davy brought us both out to meet Captain Hima, offered us a job trawling salvage out of the valley ruins.

It's been probably four years now that I've been spending my summers on Hima's rusty boat, and in that time, the guys aboard have become the closest thing I have to a family. Stoff, I – well, he's a good friend. I'd do anything for him. *Anything.*

Hours pass in mud, in water, dives broken only by tank-swaps and a lunch of pemmican wads made from wild turkey meat, honey, manzanita berries and chokecherries. When dusk comes, it's beers and *catch of the day.* The hibachi on deck burns the sky with thick, black smoke, runs with grease, but the fresh caught bass on the grill smell better than anything I can remember eating when I was human. Other than the generators, over the course of seven dives, we dredge up a pair of restorable V6 engines, ninety-two feet of 72/7 ACSR cable, seven plastic-wrapped, new-in-box laptops and about two hundred and eighty pounds of questionable canned food. All and all, a good day.

Ray cooks while the rest of us strip out of our diving suits, dry off with rough-cut sheets of canvas, enjoy the feel of the final few rays of sun as they caress our skin. After dinner, Davy does the dishes, scrubs them in the low-flow of the rusty sink in the trawler's engine room. Captain Hima calls me over to the fore of the ship, unrolls his weather-beaten map of the Valley-That-Was and together we discuss the details of the day to come, pick fish out of our teeth with the bones from the meal.

Night falls heavy and dark around us as we talk, trade ideas. The sky above opens, becomes depthless, void washed with stars. The only light comes from the trawler, from the interior fluorescents and the Christmas lights hung along the sides of the ship. The sound of Stoff and Yuri tuning a pair of old acoustics, laughing on the tail end of some unheard joke brings a certain comfortable ambiance to the settling dark. Ray brings the captain and I a couple of mystery beers, brown bottles with no labels, and we crack them open, spend a few minutes trying to guess the brands, the flavors. When Yuri finally starts to sing some off-color folk-thing about a girl he once knew, the captain grins, slaps me on the back, follows me as I make my way toward the aft of the salvage trawler, toward the music, toward the only group of guys I've ever felt any kind of kinship with. Uigenna we may be in blood, and The Rift may be Uigenna land, but we're not Uigenna in spirit, in soul. Our hearts are with the Valley-That-Was, with Cinder Hill and the rural towns among the inland swamps, the Gold Country, the hills long ago hollowed by man with his lust for the wealth hidden in the Earth.

As hara, we're different, and we realize it. We're different *together,* all trying to recapture some semblance of our humanity in a post-human age, and Cinder Hill is far enough off the beaten path, just isolated enough among the hills and mountains for us to get away with it. Some of us from the hollow hills call ourselves the Thuulhuum, after the old name for the land around Cinder Hill, but beyond all the names, all the tribal affiliations, we are, first and foremost, *brothers.* Hara-men, all cut from the same coarse cloth, just trying to get by. Always just trying to get by.

And as Stoff starts to sing his own song, we pick up the chorus together, fill the night with our voices, our music. Human, hara or something else – it doesn't matter in the moment. Only the moment itself matters. Only the music, the kinship, the night, the stars.

Terra Incognita

Nunavut

Kheops

Duwamish

Carmine City ○

Uigenna

Galhea ●

● Fulminar

Varr

● Payati

Gebaddon Ahmouth

Cinder Hill

New Milo

● Orense

Phesbe ●

Gold Country

Disputed Territories

● Imbrilim

Rift of the
Damned

Casa Ricardo ○

Greenling ●

The Ocean
of Fire

Sarroc

Karibee
Sea

P

Saltrock ●

Ouana Island

Disputed
Territories

H ✦ N

Kakkahaar

E

megalithica

CHAPTER 2

Stoff and I are sitting in a pair of aluminum folding chairs, sharing silence over mystery beers when Yuri finally packs away his guitar, spreads a sleeping bag out on the deck of the trawler. Ray and Captain Hima have already retired, maybe an hour ago, and to the same cabin, but we don't talk about it. What a man does to get some relief from the ache that comes with being a man is his own business in these post-human times. None of us has seen or been with a woman since we were human. It's another thing we don't talk about much.

Davy seems to wake up a little when Yuri stops playing. It takes him a minute to pry his ass loose from the chair near the heat of the hibachi, but when he finally does, he stumbles to the midship staircase, descends to the engine room where he's got a hammock full of quilts hanging off the wall.

I'm tired, and I can see from the look in Stoff's eyes that he's tired too, but something keeps us awake, keeps us sitting side-by-side, watching the endless void of the sea, the brilliant spray of stars shining in the blackness above. I look back at Yuri, at the bundle in the darkness that I know is Yuri, and then I turn back to Stoff, take a pull from my beer.

"Figure out what brand yours is yet?" I ask.

Stoff seems to come back from somewhere a million miles away, lifts his bottle just a little, looks at it.

"Tastes imported," is all he says.

"Yeah," I nod. "Mine too. German?"

"Maybe," he offers.

"What were you thinking about, just now?" I ask.

"Pussy," he says evenly, casually. I nod, look away in the silence that follows, look out over the sea.

Pussy. Now I'm thinking about pussy too. Been a long time, but that just makes it worse, makes you almost hallucinate the smell, the slickness of it when you think about it. Hard not to think about pussy after a long day of dives, after a couple of beers and the kinds of dirty songs that Yuri likes to play.

The feel, the sensation of my har genitals changing and hardening brings me back, brings my mind to things less pleasant. Everything down there still works now that I'm har, but it works *different*. When it gets hard, I feel like a man, but there are times when it all goes *inward*, when I start looking at guys like Stoff and Davy, start fantasizing about their hard, sleek chests, the muscles of their arms, what they'd feel like. . . what they'd feel like *inside* me.

It's weird. I've never gotten used to *that* side of myself. I know it's there, and lord knows I've indulged it a few times, but only a few. Only when the yearning gets too strong, when I'm alone with another guy and he's feeling the same way and no matter how hard we try we can't resist it.

I shake my head, try to put those thoughts out to sea. I never was a faggot, always liked girls when I was human, but as a har. . .

There's just something about being neither male or female. Something *weird*. Something I've never confronted, never really explored too much. Far as I see it, I'm male. My brothers are male, and the little indiscretions we share in the dark when need becomes too much to deny are just. . . well, they're just that. *Indiscretions.*

"You know, I knew this girl back in Monteca, back before everything went to shit," Stoff says suddenly, his eyes lost in the stars. I come back from my own thoughts, pull in a deep breath, stretch a little, take a slug from my beer as he continues. "Did I tell you about her?"

"Which one? The blond? The girl with the snake tattoos?" I ask.

"Nah," he says. "The redhead. The one with the beat-up station wagon."

"Nord *Osprey*? Fifty-six, four banger?"

"Yeah, that's the one."

"You told me about her once, I think." I pause, nurse the beer again as the tale comes back to me. "Met her at Block Video, went on a couple of dates. Real wild child, if I remember correctly." I look at him. "That the one that was into whips and paddles and stuff?"

"Yeah," he grins a little. "We was only together about a month or two, but I still think about her." He breathes, takes a pull from his beer in the pause, then offers, "You'd-a liked her, Tyse. Fun smile, sexy ass, always running around in jeans, no underwear."

No underwear. The visual he's spinning makes me hard again, fills my mind with images of his cute little redhead, what she might have looked like. I lick my lips a little, unconsciously. Stoff catches it, smiles, drowns his own thoughts in beer.

"You think there might still be women like that out there somewhere?" I ask, hesitate, then look at him, meet his eyes again. "Red hair, jeans, no underwear?"

"God, I hope so," he breathes, shakes his head. "Hell, any woman would do for me at this point. Been so long, I'd fuck a rusty hole in a steel wall if it was wet enough."

Any woman.

That's when it happens. That's when things *change* again. The hardness is gone, the distension. I'm so into my own thoughts, I hardly notice the difference until I shift in my seat, feel the eager slickness between my thighs. *Any woman.* Part of *me* is woman. Part of me yearns for the contact, for the attention, yearns to feel the heat, the stiff, *hungry–*

And then he looks at me, Stoff, and I swear he can see the thoughts in my eyes. I don't look beyond his stare, but I'm certain his male-parts are stiff and willing, bulging beneath his own faded jeans. *You could have him,* I realize, and I swallow against the thought, the urge. He doesn't have any of the curves of a woman, the soft breasts, the full lips, the hips – and yet that doesn't matter. He's *perfect.* He's exactly what my body desires, what my body needs.

And yet. . .

I clear my throat, look away. That's all it takes, all it takes to shatter the moment, bring back the stars and the balmy breezes blowing in off the sea. Between my thighs, the har-parts shift a little, uncertain, seem to settle into something more neutral, less *defined,* less eager.

No one denies that inception, that becoming har has changed us, made us into something more than human, but to me, Stoff will always be another man. He's a drinking buddy, a guy to trade stories about old girlfriends with. I can't let him be anything else. I can't let him become anything more. I may be har, but in my own mind, I'm still a man.

Sometimes I wonder if the reason we're still as good of friends as we are is because we haven't been *that way* with each other yet. I've been with Captain Hima once, a long time ago, and Davy and I – well, there was that one time when we bumped uglies in the engine room. It was quick, damn quick. I remember closing my eyes, trying to imagine it was one of my old girlfriends bucking hard against my hips instead of Davy, but meetings like that always come at a cost. We're brothers, all of us, but I don't drink or swap stories much with Davy or Hima anymore. The silences, the words between words – they're just too uncomfortable now, too awkward, too tainted with memories of what we've done, the fear that we *both* might have *enjoyed it*, that it might happen again.

Just working through the urges, I tell myself, take another slug of beer. The world is like prison now, empty of women, but a man still has *urges*.

Stoff stirs uncomfortably next to me, cups his hands around his beer, holds it over his crotch like he's trying to hide a boner. I try not to think about it, put the whole mess of sex out of my head.

Bed, I tell myself. It's getting late. Stoff and I are the only ones still awake, and we're drunk enough that if one of us doesn't go to bed soon, something just might happen. Something neither of us will be able to forget or take back. I pull in a deep breath, lean forward to rise, bracing myself against the chair.

"Well," I begin, but I never get a chance to finish.

"Hey–" he says, and that's as far as he gets. Light flickers and flashes behind us. He stands, points, but I see the meteor almost the same instant he does, watch it cut a flaming arc across the sky, come down in the water, splash close enough to rock the boat with the waves from the impact. Instantly, I'm on my feet. The fatigue is gone, stripped away, replaced with cold, with adrenaline. I stumble as I sprint for the trawler's open-air bridge, grip the edge of the door, lean into the controls. Hands jam the throttle, and I grit teeth as the engines roar to life, propellers whipping water, swinging the boat toward the fallen star. Glancing back, I see Stoff standing with arms tense, half crouched, face uncertain. I throw a quick, loose gesture at him, shout:

"Get me a tank! A suit!"

CHAPTER 3

We rarely dive at night. I can count on one hand the number of times I've been down in the Valley-That-Was after dark. Usually, it only happens when we hit a site with a lot of potential near the end of a lean week, push our dives until the last minute trying to make up the difference. Even with a flashlight, visibility is shit at night, and although none of us has ever seen any evidence of anything *dangerous*, any kind of large, hungry, predatory marine life in the sea of the Valley-That-Was, it's hard not to get the heebie-jeebies a hundred feet underwater, when all you can see is the little window of black and murky void directly in front of your face.

Before we even reach the splashdown spot, Captain Hima is on deck, shouting, confused and angry. Stoff crosses to him, puts a hand on his chest, calmly explains what's going on, what we've seen. My eyes follow the glow of the fallen star, watch as it turns from molten white to yellow, then boils off into red. I push the boat harder, grit my teeth as the bow rises and splashes over waves – got to get as close as I can before the star cools, before the glow is gone and we have to wait for morning to *maybe* find it. Even pushing the engines hard, we barely make it. By the time I lock the controls up, strip, yank on my wetsuit and strap a tank to my back, the star is little more than a hazy red stain hanging in the depths of the dark waters.

I don't wait. Stoff tosses me a flashlight, a radio, and then I'm in the water, swimming hard for that fading glow. I don't think about how hot the thing will be when I reach it, don't think about anything *except* reaching it. The closer I get, the more the water heats up, goes from cold to simmering, and it happens so suddenly that I can't help but stall a little, float, track the beam of the flashlight across the fallen star.

It's a long way down, even still, I realize. Like some couch-sized boulder, the fallen star sits in the center of a parking lot, a halo of shattered asphalt separating it from the silt that covers the rest of the seafloor. Briefly, I think about how I'm going to get it out of the water, how I'm going to get it back to the boat – and then the glow finally dies, leaves the rock black, virtually indistinguishable from the pavement, from the mud beyond it.

I risk a glance back at the boat. The trawler's lights make a hazy halo barely visible in the darkness above, but it's enough to orient myself with. Five clicks on the radio button and a minute later the winch hits the waves, sinks. I rise to catch it, then turn my flashlight back to the rock, hook the cable to my belt and swim down to the parking lot.

The water around the fallen star is hot, almost too hot to swim through. I push on anyway, reach for the rock, wrap the winch cable around it like a bow around a huge box. It hurts. It hurts a lot. The water isn't boiling, but it's close. By the time I get the thing all bound up in the winch cable, I'm eager to put some space between me and the star. Flippers churn silt, hurl me skyward, and then I'm hitting the radio again, five times.

The winch is quick. I chase it to the surface, reach the side of the trawler almost the instant the rock comes sizzling out of the water. The other guys are all wide-eyed and frantic, pointing at the meteorite, pushing in around Ray as he swings the winch over to the aft of the boat, lowers it to a point just short of the deck. By the time Stoff helps me out of the water, I'm shaking with exhaustion, and as he takes the light from me, he catches sight of my reddening skin, the blisters already rising across the backs of my hands. "Jesus Christ," he says. "Damn, Tyse. You okay?"

"No worse than a sunburn," I manage, but I let him help me out of the suit anyway, lean into his shoulder as he leads me to the below-decks hallway where a bench and a first-aid kit serve as our medbay. Chatter chases us down the stairs, echoes through the hull. I catch bits and pieces, chunks of sentences, words. Speculation, questions, snatches of half-remembered articles read on the internet when it was still a part of daily life – everyone is excited, everyone thinks the fallen star could be valuable. I know the truth – if it's stone, it probably won't be worth much. If it's iron, nickel, one of those pretty ones full of gemstones, it could be worth a fortune.

"Hold still," Stoff tells me, and I think of my mother. Soft hands touch mine, squeeze chalky antibacterial lotion onto skin, and for a moment, I can almost see the woman in Stoff. I swallow, look up at him, look at his dirty hair, his strong shoulders, will myself to see him as a man again, as a brother. It works, but he slows a little, almost as if he can sense the struggle in me, almost as if he *knows*.

"Damn lucky, seeing that thing come down," he says.

He's right. In all my life, I've only seen one other shooting star touch down close enough to *feel*. The last one was when I was a boy, when I was still human, and though, for days afterward, I searched the field where I thought it fell, I never found any trace of it. This is the first fallen star I've seen up close that wasn't locked behind glass in a museum, the first one I've been able to *touch.*

"Probably just a bag of trash some cosmonaut kicked out into orbit decades ago," I joke, but already I know it's something far more valuable than space garbage. It retains heat like steel, has weight to it. Even if it's just stone, it might be full of crystals or tiny diamonds.

The talk upstairs dies down, and then I hear the sudden snarl of a concrete saw on deck. I start, but Stoff holds me back, looks up as Ray peeks down the stairs at us.

"They cutting it open?" I ask quickly.

Ray nods, hangs off the railing like a monkey. "Hima wants–"

There's a squeal, a grinding shriek, and then I hear Davy curse as the saw goes silent. Ray glances back up the stairs, takes a step or two up toward the deck, stares.

"What happened?" I ask.

Ray glances back at us. Stoff wraps my hands with gauze, checks my face, my arms, goes into the first aid kit for something else.

"Fucking *broke my saw!*" Davy shouts.

Answers that question. Ray grins, shrugs. I can't help but laugh, shake my head. In another moment, Ray's back on deck, and it's just me and Stoff in the hall again. His hands work the top off an aerosol can full of some kind of sunburn remedy. It stings as he sprays it on, smells like plastic and disinfectant, but the cold that lingers in its wake feels good, makes me shiver.

Conversation, muffled by the decks. Someone spits, then more cursing from Davy. I look up to meet Stoff's eyes again, but he doesn't notice, doesn't meet my stare until he's through, until he's done checking me over. I manage a lopsided grin, and he smiles a little in return, socks me in the shoulder just lightly, just playfully. The first aid kit goes back on the wall, and as I stand, he reaches out to support me. Captain Hima is talking, voice even, quiet, too quiet to hear. When Stoff and I finally make it to the top of the stairs, Hima looks our way, nods once, adds: "We should wait, pick this up again in the morning."

"You okay?" Davy asks. Even with the gruff, grumbling tone, there's concern in his voice. I hold up my bandaged hands, let light catch the liquid sheen on my burnt skin. Captain Hima looks back at the fallen star suspended a few feet from the deck, a shining cut glinting in its pitted surface.

"Looks metal," I say, catch Hima's eyes, gesture at the mark where the concrete saw bit in. "That's a good sign. Could be worth a lot."

"If we can find a buyer," Davy grumbles, levers muscle into a wrench seated on the side of the saw, breaks loose the bolt holding what's left of the shattered blade.

"We'll find a buyer," Yuri says, folds his arms over his chest. "Even if Sunday's market is a bust, it'll give us a chance to get the word out. Eventually we'll get a good offer."

Davy sneers, yanks at what's left of the saw blade until it comes free, then hurls the pieces into the darkness beyond the trawler. In the silence, Hima's eyes meet mine again and he clears his throat.

"In any case, we've still got a day of dives tomorrow." The captain looks at Ray, at Yuri. The latter nods, arms drifting back to his sides. Ray just watches, only glances at Davy when the guy curses again, kicks the saw across the deck with a single solid, steel-toed blow. Hima's eyes narrow just the barest amount as he lifts his chin, and then his hands come together behind his back. "Let's get some rest. Tyse did right by us tonight, but we still need our bread-and-butter salvage to trade for bio-diesel and booze at Cinder Hill."

His eyes dart back to mine and I smile slightly, nod once. Glancing back at Yuri, at Ray, the captain unclasps his hands then, breathes, and the rest of the guys take it as a signal. Tired movements carry Davy, Ray and Cap below decks, while Yuri and I stretch out on opposite sides of the cooling hibachi. Stoff is the last one to roll out a sleeping bag, and as I turn to watch him, I see his lithe, subtly strong frame silhouetted against the fluorescents of the trawler. He looks at me, but I can't see his eyes, his lips, can only imagine he smiles at me as he reaches into the fusebox, kills the lights.

CHAPTER 4

Whirr. Dzwit-zwit. Whirrrrrrrrr.

Darkness. Scattered shards of memories from childhood rising and falling with the rhythm of the sea. I wake while it's still dark, wake with the aches of a bad dream still lingering in my shoulders, my neck. Somewhere nearby, I can hear Stoff's soft snoring, hear the quiet, quick breaths that Yuri draws in his sleep. The sea is silent – not even the sound of a night bird crying on the wind. Nothing unusual. It's always quiet at night on the sea of the Valley-That-Was.

Quiet. Dark. Makes sleep easy. Usually, I sleep like a log, sleep so deeply that I don't dream, but tonight – some nights, tonight included, I dream.

When I was human, I used to dream more often. Bad dreams, mostly – dreams about getting caught with a bag of cocaine hidden under the seat of my bike on one of the rare delivery runs I did for cash on the side in those days. Dreams about running out of gas on a long, dusty road a million miles from anywhere. Dreams about catching a friend with his dick in my girlfriend, everybody grinning, laughing, she whispering about how much better he was, how worthless a lay I am. The monsters of adulthood, mundane and yet still terrifying to behold. Far more terrifying than any shining alien or toothy demon that ever chased me through any of my childhood dreams.

Thinking about those dreams, those older dreams, I knead hard fingers into muscles, close my eyes, turn over onto my side. I can't remember much of tonight's bad dream – just shadows, a sense of urgency, a sense of something being off, *wrong*. Shifting, I bury my face into the stiff pile of old clothes that serves as my pillow, try to ignore the smell of stale sweat and mold that rises from between layers of fabric as I shift.

And then I hear it, and the dream comes back like a flash of light in the dark.

Whirr. Dzwit-zwit. Whirrrrrrrrr.

Eyes open. Legs, sharp and spider-like, aluminum and jointed with rubber. That's what I remember from the dream. Something alien, something mechanical. The star – the fallen star sloughing off burnt skin, sprouting legs, tearing itself loose from the winch –

The rattle of chains is all it takes. In an instant, I'm up, sprinting across the deck of the trawler, tearing open one of the faded orange supply chests where we keep our flashlights. Hands catch cold plastic, thumb jamming the rubbery button, painting the star with light. For a moment, all I can do is stare, *watch*, but nothing happens. *Nothing.* The star is silent, hanging there in the winch cable without moving, without any indication of life.

In the darkness, I hear Stoff snort, sigh, turn over. I breathe, thumb the flashlight off, set it back in the supply chest. A cool breeze tickles the sweat from my skin as I cross back to my sleeping bag, crouch, hesitate for a moment, listen for the sounds, the mechanical noises I could swear were coming from the fallen star only seconds before. Measuring my breaths, keeping them soft, quiet, I wait, but nothing comes. No sound, no movement. *Nothing.*

Reluctantly, I slip back into the sleeping bag. Yuri is snoring now, the sound rising, deepening, turning into something like the snarl of a saw grinding through wet wood. Eventually, Stoff wakes enough to yell something incoherent at him, and then there is silence again. *Silence.* Not even a whisper of noise from the meteorite.

At some point, I drift off. It happens suddenly – one minute I'm listening to the night, waiting for some sign or sound from the fallen star and the next, it's dawn. I look up at the red-gray sky, see Yuri's back, his ass as he drops his crusty jeans, takes his morning piss over the side of the boat. Turning over onto my back, I stare up at the endless sky, the broken, cottony cloud cover rippling through the gray. Another cool morning before the heat of a summer day on the sea of the Valley-That-Was.

"Friday," Stoff says, breathes. Yuri is whistling now, hikes up his jeans, shakes a few drops of piss from his dick-thing, lets them fall on the weathered deck. I turn to look at Stoff, find him blinking, rubbing the crust out of his eyes, blinking again. *Friday.* I pull in a long, deep breath. *Last day of dives before the market.*

I half consider asking Stoff how he slept, if he heard anything in the night, but before I can, he pushes himself upright, stretches creaking arms, legs, stands with his back to me, eyes toward the sun, toward the hazy ridges of distant mountains. In the silence, I hear Yuri clear his throat, hear the splat as phlegm hits water. Another moment, and I push myself into a sitting position, wait until Stoff turns back, crouches down to roll up his sleeping bag. I look at him then, and he looks at me, but neither of us speaks. A question hangs the pause, the expectation of an answer without having to ask for it, but neither of us breaks the silence. When Stoff finally rises, stuffs his bedroll into a space between two orange supply chests, I look away, look toward the fallen star, force myself to stand, to face the day.

Davy, Ray and Hima rise a handful of minutes after

those of us on deck do. In the break, I stare at the sea. According to the map, we're probably near the edge of the no-man's land between Stock Town and Monteca. French Camp is maybe a few miles to the south. Nothing there but a few ruined houses, a septic tank manufacturer, farm fields long ago drowned, sunken in silt.

Before the fallen star, Captain Hima had talked about hitting the dark tangle of steel and aluminum that had been the naval supply annex on the western edge of Stock Town, seeing what we could dredge up from the warehouses there before moving north again after lunch. Wouldn't be the first time we've tried the annex. Might be the first time we find something other than steel cable and decorative gravel in the thick slurry of liquid cardboard and trash that hangs like a gelatinous beast over the seafloor there. Not the best way to end a week, but who knows – Hima's hunches turn out to be worthless only a little less often than they turn out to be golden.

Next week, though – for next week, Hima had suggested we might take a break from routine and follow the meandering coast as far as the marshlands around Napa Bay. Not the safest territory, always the risk of running into gangs of feral hara or humans squatting in some of the old hilltop wineries still on dry land, but the grapes that clog the swamps will be heavy with fruit soon, and we might even be able to bring enough wine out of the drowned vineyards and stores in deeper waters to make the trip worth the extra cost in bio-diesel. A trip out to Napa Bay and back usually takes two weeks, means we have to take on extra dry goods, break out the guns, but being able to eat your fill of wild swamp grapes, drink as many glasses as you can hold of the finest cabernet sauvignon humanity ever bottled – it's worth it. One of the things that makes life worth living in a time so full of the reminders of how easy it is to die.

The sound of Ray breaking out breakfast brings me back. Loose, tired, we all gather around last night's find. More pemmican, half a can of cling peaches in syrup for each of us. When we're done, the paper plates go into the hibachi – starter for tonight's dinner.

Stretches come first. Simple stuff, a routine Hima and Yuri came up with at some point before Stoff and I joined the trawler's crew. Squats, lunges, the kinds of moves that keep you limber, pop the sleep out of your muscles. Halfway through, Davy passes me a bottle of cheap, hearty cider brewed from manzanita berries back at Cinder Hill. It's thick, sweet, burns on the way down, but keeps you warm while you're working underwater. I take a slug, then another, pass the bottle to Stoff and then drop back into a hamstring stretch. A handful of minutes later and the workout group breaks apart, Hima going to the controls, kicking the trawler into a steady cruise, carrying us out over the naval supply annex while we pull on our diving suits, check our oxygen tanks. Ray tops us off, checks our gear. I rub my skin down with a dollop of antibacterial lotion, pull on gloves. The trawler coasts to a stop and I put one foot up on the edge, look down at the shadows of the trash-choked warehouses below.

Another day, another set of dives.

And even as I dive into the water, my mind goes back to the dreams, the sounds, the mechanical noises the meteorite might have made in the night.

CHAPTER 5

The water above the naval supply annex is murky, almost too murky to see through. Gloved hands paw through the darkness, paw through mud and trash, find nothing. For three dives, we find nothing. So many of the boxes in the warehouses have disintegrated, their fragile contents soaked and turned to paste. No idea what any of the stuff was before the water covered Stock Town, but we all have theories. Cup ramen, Davy thinks. Cases and cases of cup ramen. Foam sealant is Stoff's guess, maybe some kind of glue. Yuri says powdered milk, maybe powdered potatoes, flour, that kind of thing. Could be any of those things – it's that thick down here. It's like swimming through cold chowder.

Fourth dive is when we finally find something worth winching back. Big crate on a pallet – turns out to be car parts. Electrical components mostly. Distributor caps, fuses, boxes of spark plugs and solenoids, that kind of thing. Thing is heavy, and the roof overhead is intact, all corrugated iron. Cargo doors to the warehouse are jammed, all too far away from the crate anyway. Davy makes a gesture, hits the radio call button three times. A few moments later, Ray tosses a cable overboard, the whole thing sinking fast, weighed down by the bulky rig of an underwater cutting torch. Stoff and I circle back, help Davy with the rig, guide him with gestures, then avert our eyes as he cuts an egress hole in the roof of the warehouse, lets the chunk of iron fall into the muck.

Three more clicks on the radio, a long pause, and then five more. Yuri chases the cutting torch back to the surface, watches it, supports it as Ray draws it in, then tosses the winch hook overboard. It takes all of Davy's, Stoff's and my strength to move the chunk of roof aside, and almost the instant we push the thing clear, Yuri brings us the hook, helps us secure it to the crate.

Lunch comes after the fourth dive. Being the Friday of a good week, Hima breaks out the treats he's been saving since Monday. This week, it's chunks of roasted rattlesnake dripping with a glaze of bay laurel nut, pepper and honey that almost tastes like teriyaki. A couple of dusty candy bars split amongst us rounds out the meal, and as we sit on the deck picking the last few bits of rattlesnake out of the foil wrapper it was roasted in, Hima starts up the trawler, sets us on a lazy, northerly course.

We only get in two more dives before Hima calls it a day. The spot he stops the trawler over is a shadowy pit that was once a marina sandwiched between a subdivision and a long, flat stretch of silt, probably the remains of a rice paddy. Underwater, old covered docks sag into the darkness, and as we search for anything useful that might have been loaded onto one of the many thrashed and silt-covered boats clustered at the bottom of the pit, the beams of our lights bounce off shining hulls, cast weird and ominous shadows through the murky depths. Our hauls are light, armloads brought to the side of the boat, handed off to Ray and Hima. Trinkets, lunchbox-coolers crammed with old sodas or beers. Stoff finds a closet crammed with clothes sealed up in plastic, "space-saver" vacuum bags. A couple of nice suits, a couple of dresses, lots of winter clothes – all fresh, clean, dry. Most of what I find is useless – bags of chips, trail mix, junk food mushed and spoiled by the water. A couple of rings pulled off fingers picked free of flesh by fish are the highlights of my last dive. Davy tells me one looks like diamond, speculates that the others are just gold with some glass or crystal stones in them. Pocket change for the market, Hima says, grinning. He's right. I might be able to trade the diamond one for a meal, the others for some beers at Servente's in Cinder Hill. Better than nothing.

When we come back from our last dive, the hibachi is already smoking. *Catch of the day* again, trout this time, fennel and rosemary for seasoning. Davy and I opt for mystery beers again, but Hima, Ray and Yuri go through a couple of bottles of champagne that had been sitting in a fridge aboard one of the yachts in the sunken marina. By the time the sky is dark and lit with stars, we're almost all rip-roaring drunk – and that's when I ask Stoff about it. The meteorite, the whirring in the middle of the night.

At first he's only half paying attention. We're all distracted by Yuri, by the broken rendition of a classic rock tune he's singing, a tune we all only half remember. Ray and Hima offer lines to supplement Yuri's own, and it isn't long before the song seems to take on a life of its own, seems to segue into another song's chorus, then another's. Between lines, I try to get Stoff's attention, but it's only when I start telling him about the dream that he looks up, meets my eyes evenly.

"It – it sprouted legs?" he asks, blinks.

"In the dream, yeah," I nod. "When I woke up, there was this mechanical noise. Did you hear it?"

"During the night?" he asks, trying to focus.

"Yeah," I respond. In the pause, Stoff just looks at me, stares but doesn't say anything. Without our voices in the mix, the song falters a little. Yuri's smile slips as he gets distracted by our sudden seriousness, the way Stoff is suddenly staring at the couch-sized meteorite crouching under a net of steel cable at the far aft end of the ship. Davy glances over at us, just for an instant before he gets swept up in the song again, but his eyes follow Stoff as he stands, crosses the deck to the fallen star.

"You didn't hear it last night?" I ask, join him beside the meteorite.

"I didn't hear much of anything," Stoff hesitates, eyes studying the burnt and pitted surface, the gleaming chrome where Davy's saw bit into metallic skin. "I slept like a brick."

"You woke up to yell at Yuri."

"For snoring again?" he asks.

"Yeah."

"Don't remember it, but okay." He reaches out, stops, gently brushes fingers against the meteorite, traces the line of the steely wound. Looking up at me again, he adds, "You sure the noise wasn't just part of your dream?"

"I'm sure," I nod, turn my eyes back to the fallen star. "I was awake when I heard it. Wasn't any kind of sound you ever hear out here on the water."

"Not any kind of sound you'd expect from a space rock," he says. It's half question, half statement.

I shake my head. "No, not that I know of."

"What about gas?" He glances back at me. "Some kind of ice inside maybe melting. . ."

He lets the sentence trail off. I turn my eyes back to the fallen star, lick my lips. Bits of the dream come back to me, visions of alien malice in stiff, steely movements. *Silly shit*, I tell myself. *No such thing as aliens. Just a rock. Gonna be worth a lot of money.*

"How much you think it'll fetch?" Hima asks, stops beside me. Stoff and I look over, find him grinning back at us, but it doesn't stick. "What's wrong?" He finally asks.

Stoff opens his mouth to say something, but I shake my head, cut him off. "Nothing. Nothing's wrong." I pause, consider. "Just had a weird dream last night." I glance back at the meteorite. "Weird dream about the rock."

"Yeah?" Hima prompts, but I don't respond, give him only a gesture that says it doesn't matter. He pulls in a deep breath, nods, turns his eyes back to the rock.

"If it's like that all the way through," I gesture at the cut in the surface of the fallen star, "we could probably trade it for something big. Fifty gallons of kerosene, hundred of bio. Solar kit for the trawler, maybe."

"Solar would be nice," Hima nods, puts his hands in his pockets.

"Would make longer trips easier," Stoff puts in. "Just food and booze to budget."

"Gonna take some talking, though," I add, glance up, meet Hima's eyes. "Most folks back at Cinder Hill won't have the tools to do anything with it. Smith up in Coluton probably will, probably know the value of it too, but won't have much on hand to trade for it."

Hima nods. "If we can't find a good offer at the market, I'll see what I can arrange. Might take a few days in town, but if we can convert the trawler to solar, it'd be worth the downtime."

"Think you can get 'ol Bill Hastings over at the Cinder Hill Inn to bankroll the smith?" Stoff asks.

"Him or the brewer at the north end of the main drag." Hima glances at Stoff. "Maybe both."

"They'll want a cut," I offer.

"Then let's hope it sells off the tailgate on Sunday." Hima nods again, turns, offers a fresh smile. "Plenty of time to think about money when we're on the ground again. Rock might make us rich, might turn out we can't find anyone who will take it for anything more than a song or a can of bad beer. Whatever happens, hell of a find, Tyse." He claps a hand across my shoulder then, lets it linger a little too long. I look away, swallow, look back, force a nod.

"Want another beer?" Stoff asks. His words don't reach me immediately – my eyes, my mind follow Hima back to the Hibachi, back to Yuri and Davy and Ray. Something in his movements, in the way he walks, the way he smiles, slides in so effortlessly next to Ray triggers a rush within me, brings memories bubbling up, memories of a night when I slept in his arms, felt the slick heat between his thighs –

I swallow reflexively, push the thoughts out of my mind. When I turn back, Stoff is looking at me. I blink, shake my head. "What?"

"Beer," he holds up his empty bottle. "Want another one?"

"Sure," I manage, then add, just as he's walking away, "one of those green bottles Davy found today, if we've got any more in the cooler."

"Yep," is all Stoff says.

CHAPTER 6

Saturday breakfast on the trawler is always something sweet. This week, it's a toasted acorn bread slathered with a jam made from dogwood berries. The greasy smoke of the hibachi makes the bread taste a little more savory than it does when it's eaten cold, and we take our time with it while Hima sets us drifting east at a lazy pace. The shadows of Stock Town pass slowly beneath us, buildings and homes blurring into dark patches divided by long, straight lanes of mud, and slowly, so slowly, the bottom comes closer, rises along the shallow slope of an east-rising hill. Only when we reach the tangled iron and concrete reef that pokes out here and there amongst the saltwater bayou at the edge of the sea of the Valley-That-Was does Hima cut the throttle to just short of nothing, thread the trawler through the ruins of east Stock Town. The shadows of old Highway Four are the target, and Hima lines the boat's prow up perfectly, follows the sunken road in toward the shore.

The land beside the Four is all flat and silent, muddy and dark under about six or ten feet of water. Broken trees jut from the silt here and there, mark high spots among the little islands that were once hills. Certain landmarks guide us – a pair of hilltop houses once owned by farmers, now burnt and broken, jutting like blackened crowns from the crests of sunken hills. Most of the land that rolls on beneath the trawler was pasture in the years before, cattle land, sparsely treed, empty for miles.

The place Hima picks to make landing is just north of another house, another ruin. Twisted knots of barbed wire fencing jut up around the trawler as he nudges it just short of the shore, sticks it into a swampy wodge of brush and branches. Yuri ties one end of a thick, braided rope to the side of the boat, ties the other to his belt, then dives into the morass, swims through driftwood and floating cruft until he reaches the shore. A telephone pole, snapped in half by the ferocity of some long-forgotten storm, juts from the water at an awkward angle, makes the perfect point for Yuri to anchor the ship to.

And that's when the rest of us get to work.

Part of surviving in The Rift of the Damned is knowing how to protect yourself. As a precaution, every one of us carries a knife, and Hima keeps a pair of beat-up old twenty-two caliber rifles in his cabin, but we can't take the boat with us to Cinder Hill, and no amount of firepower will protect your assets when you're not around to watch them.

The solution is simple, ingenious. There's an art to hiding your valuables in plain sight. The swampy thicket where we park the trawler is virtually identical to a dozen others crowded along the shore, and with Davy's cunning use of an impact wrench, the trawler itself looks like it's been sitting abandoned for decades, just collecting rust. The plates and bolts he removes go with us, come together to make the disassembled frame of a pair of high-sided trailers.

When we leave, we take everything with us. Food, fuel, salvage, guns, personal belongings – the boat is just a shell when we're done. A pair of deep cycle batteries run the winch until the trawler is empty, and then we pull even those. Piece by piece, we drag it all to the shore, and it's almost noon by the time we get it all into a pile beside the old fire road that comes down the hillside from the ruined house where we keep our trucks.

The house itself doesn't make much of a target – anyone can tell from a long way off that it no longer has a roof, that half of it is sagging into the sea. Get closer, and the amount of coyote scat in the weeds of the front yard is sure to give any small group of feral hara or humans a scare. In small numbers, coyotes won't mess with people, but in a pack the size of the one that we've made it look like lives here, they can be very dangerous to individuals, pairs and trios.

The garage is a three-car box collapsed in the front. Looks inaccessible from the approach, but closer inspection reveals that the soggy back end is open. A pair of old trucks, dusty and buried under a couple of large chunks of roofing, seem to be worthless, nothing more than some human's forgotten hobby project. They've got no fuel in their tanks, no batteries, no wheels. We load all those bits on the trawler when we park the trucks, leave them for the week.

Takes about an hour to uncover the trucks, get them started up and rolling. Yuri walks the perimeter, checking for signs of other hara, of humans, anyone or anything that might have passed through while we were away, but finds nothing. Ray picks fruit from the loquat trees along the shore, pits them and keeps us snacking as we move. Hima helps Davy, Stoff and I get the trucks through the marshy dirt behind the garage. We take them out one by one, use old boards to get the tires through the tough spots, and once both of the vehicles are pulled up on either side of our shoreside salvage pile, we load them up. Davy assembles the trailers for the big stuff, the generators and the fallen star. The impact wrench screams as the bolts spin home, grinds as they come up tight, binding steel to steel. All in all, it's just short of two in the afternoon by the time we're ready to hit the road, take the rest of the Four inland to the hollow hills, to the Gold Country, to the land where the hara call themselves the Thuulhuum. Hima drives the lead truck in our convoy. Yuri drives the other. Stoff and I ride with the salvage in the back of Yuri's truck, grin and give salutes to Davy and Ray as Hima hits the gas, sets the pace for our journey.

In my hands, the twenty-two rifle feels heavy and necessary, but I can't say why. Our truck grumbles as Yuri starts it, and as I turn to look over the rusted and peeling roof of the cab, I see the glint of steel from the cut in the skin of the fallen star. Tied down in the trailer bouncing behind Hima's truck, it almost looks like a captive, almost makes me nervous. Good hauls always make me nervous, though. Good hauls make good targets for gangs brave enough to hit armed vehicles on the road.

Not that we've ever been hit, I tell myself. *This stretch ain't nothing like the open land further north, beyond The Rift.* The Four is usually pretty empty, has enough small communities straddling it to keep it safe.

Most of the time.

CHAPTER 7

I cast one last glance back at the ruined house, at the thicket where the Trawler waits for our return, brace myself against the bump as the truck crosses the break between dirt driveway and asphalt highway. Like a thirsty old man, the Four sags into the swamplands around us, touches the mud but always meanders away again. The long, white sheds of an old turkey farm rise up along the crest of a hill as we hit the first rolling stretch of the highway, provide a sort of landmark before we hit the soaring overlook just outside the ruins of Copperburg. A bent sign, rusted and full of holes from a brush with a shell of birdshot marks the beginning of the ascent. It's barely legible now, and I can't remember what the name of that last road before the overlook is, but I recognize the sign all the same. Can't count how many times I gunned my bike past that sign in the days when I was still human, how many times I saw it, knew I was only maybe twenty minutes from home.

Copperburg always makes me nervous. After the overlook, the highway descends down into a different stretch of swamp, curves north, then keeps going past the point where our caravan bumps off onto Oborn Ferry Road. Oborn Ferry is main street Copperburg, and even though all the buildings of that old town are nothing more than chunks of burnt wood jutting from concrete foundations now, I always feel like I'm being watched when we drive through. It's almost the perfect ambush spot. It's a bottleneck, a narrow, two-lane road with a hill on one side and a ditch beyond the ruins on the other.

E. S. Wynn

Blind entrances to roads that drop down beyond the foundations of shattered houses. A hundred hara with rifles could lay down in certain spots along the length of that in-town stretch of Oborn Ferry and we'd never even know they were there until it was too late. That's why it makes me nervous.

Hima creeps through the town, keeps us moving slow enough that the trailers don't rattle much, and we pass through without incident. If anyone's around, they don't come out for us. Makes it a typical convoy run – me, nervous, with the gun in my hands, watching every shadow until the whole town is behind us. Stoff grins at me as we pass between the last few buildings, hit open highway again. Hima hits the throttle, Yuri gunning it to catch up. Looking out the back of the truck, I watch Copperburg shrink, disappear behind a stand of oak trees as the road curves away from the town. Almost immediately, I start to feel better.

And that's when I hear Davy shout.

I can't make out the words, but as I spin, I catch his gesture, his pointing finger. My eyes track to the sky, and for a moment I don't see anything but the pale blue, the immense and cloudless emptiness. Even when I spot what he's yelling about, I don't recognize it at first. "Couldn't be," I whisper, even knowing that it is. *Airplane,* or something like it. Something black, high up, cutting a sharp line across the sky. Whatever it is, it's silent, so silent – doesn't roar like the high-altitude recon planes that used to cruise over the house I grew up in, doesn't scream like a jet. Immediately, the nervousness comes back, but also a sense of confusion, of curiosity. Airplanes disappeared with the human race, with women and late night cable. Sure, there are few hara who live out at the county airport, guys who know how to fly the old beer-can *Saginaw S-152s* and '72s, but all those birds run on straight avgas, and that's worth almost more per gallon than a month's supply of good food or clean water these days.

And none of those civilian aircraft look like the thing soaring over us now. None of them are so sleek, so black, so silent or deadly-looking. I swallow, raise my rifle, not even thinking about the fact that I'd probably have about a snowball's chance in hell of hitting the thing, but by the time I get the scope to my eye, the plane is gone. Quick as a shot – not even contrails to mark its passing.

"What in the hell?" is all Stoff can manage. I nod. *What in the hell* is right. I wrack my brain for anything I might have seen before that looks like the thing we just saw hanging in the sky above us. Nothing comes to mind. *Nothing.*

I'm still watching the sky when I feel the truck start to slow.

It's Hima first, Yuri following his lead. As a convoy, we drop back from about fifty miles an hour to a steady twenty. The reason becomes clear almost immediately – a glint on the curve of the next rise, something blue-silver, something long and rounded on the edges. A four-door sedan. In about the space of a minute, it's right on us, right where we can see it, and Davy shouts as it merges suddenly into our lane.

Hima's quick, damn quick. He jams the wheel hard to the left, but the sedan still manages to clip his truck with enough force to shear the right fender from the frame, send it exploding into the road. Blinded by a cloud of fiberglass and plastic thrown up from the collision, I almost lose my grip on the twenty-two rifle as Yuri swerves into the oncoming lane, leaves the crunched sedan spinning out in the road behind us. Quick, fluid, it turns, jerks as it tries to pursue us, fights the one bent wheel, the crumpled edge of a bumper grinding against asphalt. Before it can catch up to us, I brace myself against the cab, take aim. The scope swings across the cracked and smoking hood, rises to the spiderwebbed windshield – and that's when I hesitate. I can't see clear enough through the cracks in the glass to spot the driver, but I know where he should be. Uncertain, I line up the shot, lick my lips. *Now or never.* Fire.

The round is small, but the impact is strong enough to knock a big chunk of the glass out of the frame. Beside me, Stoff blinks. Even from here, even without a scope, he sees exactly what I see.

Nothing.

"Tyse," he starts, but he can't finish it. I shake my head. The car twitches against the centerline as it picks up speed, engine howling into redline RPMs, but no one's driving it. *No one.*

I don't know how to react. I look at the car through the scope again, brace myself as Yuri and Hima jam the trucks up to sixty, then seventy. The four-door sedan keeps up with us, and I watch as the steering wheel judders back and forth as if there were a pair of invisible hands trying to steady it. It makes no sense, terrifies me.

Almost the instant I lower the scope, Hima and Yuri slow to take a sharp corner. I glance over the roof at the road ahead, wind whipping my hair. I recognize the turn, the big oak tree there – we're getting close to the cliffside town of Blackjack, to the stretch of canyon road that twists between the mountain and a deep, cold reservoir. Not a good place to get caught in a car chase. Not a good place to be doing anything over thirty miles an hour.

When I look back, Stoff shouts – my eyes hit the sedan just in time to see it swerve around us, cut into the open lane and gun it hard for the bumper of Hima's truck. Ray raises his own twenty-two, puts a couple of holes in the hood and empty driver's seat, but it doesn't stop the sedan. Like a battering ram, the car accelerates suddenly, slams into the back of Hima's truck with enough force to send both of our guys sprawling into the salvage. Ray's rifle slips from his hands, clatters across the raised edge of the bed, barks as it hits the road. The angle of the sedan is sharp and the engine growls as it grinds its bent front bumper against the back end of Hima's truck, pushes it harder and harder toward the opposite curb. The trailer squeals against the hitch, bounces back and forth, more on one wheel than the other. Yuri sticks close to Hima for an instant, drops back a bit as if uncertain, then guns it suddenly, swipes the back end of the sedan hard enough to send it spinning over the fog line and into a tree. As I look back, I see the flicker of flames, black smoke pouring into the sky. One wheel of the sedan keeps twitching as it shrinks with the road behind us, but it's obvious the car isn't going anywhere anytime soon. I breathe, look ahead again, catch the lines of the last asphalt curve before the canyon.

And that's when *they* step out onto the road.

Four of them, hara maybe, all dressed in black and camo. No weapons we can see, but this far away and with the sun in our eyes, they're little more than silhouettes. Hima yells something, and I catch the gesture from Ray. *Get down, hold on.* He's gonna gun it through, I realize, run over anyone dumb enough to stand in his path. I drop like a rock, press my back flat against the back of the bed, brace my feet against the side of a crate packed with salvage.

I don't hear the impact, don't see it, only *feel* it. It's surreal the way time seems to slow, the way everything grinds down to a single moment where you look up and see a chunk of bent steel spinning end over end through the air. I recognize the paint immediately– that beat-up shade of off-white. The chunk of metal is from Hima's truck.

The cloud of shattered glass and shrapnel that follows it is from ours.

Stoff isn't holding on as tight as I am. I scream some wordless sound as the impact knocks him sideways, bounces his head off steel. Before I can react, reach for him, he's in the air, spinning ass-over-teakettle. He hits the road shoulder-first, barely misses the skidding tires of the trailer, and then he's gone – *gone.*

The gun is forgotten. I stand, shout after Stoff, half register the weird angle the truck is moving at. Down from up and to my left, one wheel in the air, tailgate cutting a sharp, sideways line to the curb of the road. I risk a look through the grimy back window of the truck, but everything ahead is black, is a cloud of smoke and singing shards of steel that cut air inches from my scalp. Somehow, I get down again, drop among the salvage, wrap my hands around a coil of 72/7 ACSR cable. The wire spool seems weightless in the instant before the truck slams back to the asphalt. I look to the left, see a pile of rusty fuel cans just as they rush, and then everything goes black.

When my eyes open again, I'm on the road. No memory of how I got here. Hands scratch across broken glass, road grit. The whole world seems to hum, ring like time is caught in the tolling moment of some giant bell. A dozen feet away, I see a blown tire spinning in the air, the crunched sides of an upturned trailer near it. Someone is shouting – can't tell who. Can't see anyone. One shaky hand brushes hair, comes away bloody.

And that's when I see him.

Yuri, upside down, still strapped into the driver's seat of what's left of his truck. I think it's Yuri. Has to be. Hard to tell. I blink through blurry eyes. A gleaming arch of bone juts from his shattered cheek. His skin is lost in blood, hangs from his face like the shreds of a crimson flag.

Something hits me suddenly, jars me, drags me to my feet. Can't see. Can't –

Someone is yelling in my ear. I see Hima's truck, the wad of steel that must be Hima's truck. The back tires are smoking, tailgate jutting improbably skyward, chunk of the trailer's hitch arm still hanging, the steel torn, ragged.

Hands push me, shove me. There's an arm hanging out of the wreckage of Hima's truck. I stare. More yelling, but I only shake my head.

And that's when I see it, see *him.*

When *he* rounds the wreckage, whoever has been herding me stops suddenly, leaves me standing on unsteady legs. I recognize the silhouette, the swatches of black, green and brown crawling across his angular torso. He's one of the figures from the road, one of the men or hara that Hima was going to run down. He isn't bleeding. Not a scratch on him. When he moves, he moves like a har, I note. Like a man, but heavier, his steps more even, more confident, *stronger.* Instead of a face, I see only a sleek mask of glossy black glass that catches the light as he turns to look at me.

The yelling has stopped. I barely register the silence before a hand shoves me, sends me sprawling away from the masked man. I stumble toward the debris-choked fog line of the road, turn back, lose my balance in the process. I hit the asphalt flat on my ass, look up just in time to see Davy brace one of the twenty-two rifles against his shoulder. The gun barks, flashes, and then there's a blur, a moment of movement that ends with Davy reeling, twitching. Like a vision of death, the masked man stands over him, black, thin-fingered hands half-curled, dripping with harish blood. Davy doesn't move after he hits the ground, doesn't get up.

The masked man looks at me again, then picks up the rifle, breaks it into little chunks with his inhumanly strong fingers. My eyes go wide, but he only stares at me as he does it, waits in silence. The chunks clatter and splinter as they hit the ground, and in another moment, he's gone, crossing back out of sight. In the silence that follows, my eyes go back to Davy, but I can't move. I can't *will* myself to move.

Can't say how long I sit there. The deafening squeal of bending metal brings me back, scares me to my shaking feet. Eyes dart right, dart over the upturned wreckage of Yuri's truck, the salvage scattered all across the road, the broken and bent trailer sitting cockeyed on one tire off to my left. The road is a wasteland of glass and iron, of plastic and rubber chunks. Davy's face is a mire of mangled meat without eyes, without shape. I stumble toward him, stumble forward, put a hand out to brace myself against the bent end of Yuri's truck. Pain comes back, aches in my sides, my back. I limp, shiver, but my attention is still elsewhere, is still with the gang who so effortlessly turned the tables on us. I can hear them nearby, can hear them working, but there are no voices, nothing but the creaking and rattling of steel.

It feels like it takes me an eternity to creep around the edge of the truck, to get my eyes on the men, on the hara, the *creatures*. Four of them – no more than before, no less, and none seem to be wounded. I blink, watch them as they use their hands to rip open the trailer that had been attached to Hima's truck. They either don't notice me, or they *don't care*. They seem wholly focused on tearing apart the trailer, of getting at something inside the tangle of steel and –

All at once, I realize what they're after. Thin, nimble fingers eviscerate iron grating, slash through thick tie-downs with razor efficiency. *The Star*. They have the meteorite free in a matter of seconds, and as one of the men drags it from the trailer, another steps up beside him, helps him lift it.

And then they're moving. Uncertain, terrified, I hunch down a little further against the wreckage. A noise draws my attention away, and as I glance to my left, I catch sight of Stoff, one of his arms cradled against his chest, feet hitting the pavement in an awkward limp. He doesn't seem to see the men, doesn't seem to see anything but the wreckage. Crouching, my back to the flipped truck, I gesture, finally manage to catch his attention, draw him over.

Before he can reach me, his eyes go wide and he stops, almost stumbles. I have to dart out from the cover of the truck to grab him, drag him out of sight. The men work as if nothing has changed, as if we aren't even there. Two of them carry the meteorite in impossibly strong arms while the other two stay close by, loosely following, their masked faces sweeping the massacre, never settling in one place for too long. In the pause, Stoff opens his mouth to say something, but I make a gesture emphasizing the importance of silence, point to Davy to drive my point home. Stoff nods, his whole body shaking. It's a hot day, but we're both shivering, can't stop.

CHAPTER 8

We stay there like that for a long time, don't move, just stare at one another, breath coming in ragged draws as the pain and the silence come back. The smell of fuel hangs heavy in the air, lessens as the hot summer sun dries it into the pavement. Eventually, I get thirsty. Stoff and I look at each other and I gesture, something loose that looks like I'm drinking from an invisible bottle. Stoff nods, doesn't say anything. Eventually, I work up the nerve to stand, to see what's left of our salvage caravan.

Whatever the men did to Hima's truck, there isn't much left of it. With the back end jutting toward the sky and the front crunched up almost flat, it looks like he drove it straight into a granite cliff face. There are marks all over the road, grooves in the blacktop where rushing steel bit and bounced while it slid to a stop. Pieces of Ray are spread from the truck to the trailer, a shoe with his foot still in it –

I look away again, try to focus. Everyone except me and Stoff is dead.

My legs get all shaky again, and before I can stop it, I'm leaning forward, vomiting. Stoff turns away, closes his eyes. He's hurting, I can tell. We're both hurting.

We're both damn lucky to be alive.

Wiping the bile from my chapped lips, I force myself to stand again, to look at the grisly scene. Hima's truck had the food, the bottled water, but all that, everything that was in the bed with Davy and Ray is spread from hell to breakfast. A cracked cooler propped against the opposite curb of the road a few yards from Hima's trailer catches my eye, seems promising.

Stoff watches me with worried eyes as I limp out into the road, scan the debris, check behind me. No sign of the men that hit us, no sign that they took anything other than the meteorite.

Doesn't take me long to reach the cooler. A few seconds, but I feel every step. Hands shake as I work the bent clasp loose, tear open the lid, find a morass of glass shards swimming in beer and jam.

The sound of the lid falling closed as I let go of it startles me – I'm that out of it. I'm that rattled. I glance at Stoff again, but he only stares back, doesn't gesture, doesn't say anything. Expectant, fearful – his expression is like that of a child, a boy beaten by a drunken father. I can't imagine how I look. There's blood in my hair, tracks of it dried along the skin of my face. Everything hurts. I look away, close my eyes. *Got to find water.*

I try not to look at the stains near the crunched-up cab of Hima's truck as I kick through the debris, look for something, anything that might get Stoff and I through. It's all there – all of it, all of our supplies, all the food and booze and water we either bought or dredged up from the Valley-That-Was, but most of it is trashed, scattered or tainted by broken glass. Eventually, I find a pair of well-worn plastic water bottles, both full and sealed. An old candy tin packed with acorn bread seems to be the only other thing that's still mostly in one piece. It isn't much, but it'll do. It'll get us through.

At some point, Stoff comes out of hiding, walks back along the road and scoops up the other twenty-two rifle, the one lost during the chase. It's a little beat up and the scope is broken, but it still dry-fires. Neither of us feels brave enough to test it with a live round, and even realizing how useless the gun seems to be against men like those who nearly killed us, it makes me feel safer to have it.

At some point, we notice simultaneously how late it's getting. Didn't matter until the shadows got long, the sun getting fat and red, hanging a few fingers above the horizon. Every moment since we were knocked into the road seems to have passed in a blur, in one long, disjointed film reel of broken images, unfinished ideas. Stoff and I find three more bottles of water and a couple of cans of beer that survived by some miracle, but by the time we decide to start walking, we're down to just a bottle and a half. The acorn bread goes slower. Neither of us is really hungry.

Like a couple of vagrants, we follow the road, walk beside it instead of on it until the curb disappears at the top of the winding stretch of Oborn Ferry that clings to the canyon wall of the reservoir. Neither Stoff or I talk about how far we still have to walk. The bypass that heads into Cinder Hill is twenty miles or so away. Lot of ground to cover.

More than we can manage before the night comes.

Blackjack is another Gold Country town that hasn't survived our little apocalypse. Most of the original residents were retirees, well-off enough to have their ponderous mansions built half on the canyon wall below the road, half on stilts and concrete supports. Most of the homes in Blackjack have fallen into the swollen reservoir below them since then, but a few of the newer ones still cling to the stone like ornate insects, their windows broken, some marked with Uigenna graffiti. No one lives in Blackjack anymore, or at least, no one has called it home for a long time. Not since the evacuations, at least.

The stars are out by the time we reach Blackjack. In the distance, we hear a pair of mountain lions calling to one another, screaming their quick barks, their cries that sound like someone shouting "Ouch!" over and over again. At some point, something catches a rabbit, slaughters it even as it screams, the sound like the cry of a terrified child. Stoff kicks down the rotten door of the first sturdy-looking house we spot in Blackjack, and together we make our way to a bedroom on the second story, close the door, block ourselves in with all the furniture we can find. The mattress is soft, one of those expensive foam deals, smells like mildew, like mold.

Doesn't matter. It's cold. We huddle together under musty blankets, hold each other through the night. Stoff's scent relaxes me a little, and as I pull him closer, I feel his breath in my hair, feel him bury his face in my scalp.

Somehow, we sleep. I wake up in the middle of the night to the sound of coyotes, the yipping and howling, almost sing-song chaos of a large pack not all that far away. For a long time, I lie there listening to them, listen even after they go quiet, leave the crickets to fill the silence. When sleep comes again, it comes lazy, slow, full of foggy dreams, passes in a blink. Too soon, the sun is up, the first rays of dusty yellow pouring in through blinds aged from white to beige.

Hungry, feeling all of our cuts and bruises as if for the first time, Stoff and I wake up slow. My whole body feels like a wad of knotted muscle, every inch of skin too soft, too sore to put any weight into. I try to stretch, try to move, bare teeth against the pain, ultimately plant my face into a pillow and groan. Stoff isn't much better off, but even still he reaches out to me, reaches up through the bottom of my crusty shirt and kneads his fingers into my muscles.

It hurts a little at first, feels better and better as he works on me. His hand is strong, seems to know just where to dig in. Doesn't take long before he gets a grunt out of me, then a sigh, a long, deep exhale. Like a cat, I rise under his hand, half-guide him to the tough spots with my body, shift and groan with the mixture of pleasure and pain. Lost in the moment, it's perfect. It's exactly what I need.

Somehow, we drift closer. It feels good, feels natural. I turn and look into his eyes – dark, shades of autumn brown, autumn green. Dark hair falls across his face, his nose. This close, I can almost pretend he's a woman, a beautiful woman – almost don't have to pretend.

When he kisses me, it's soft, has a strength to it. I close my eyes, but I can't kiss him back. Something about it, something about being a man, about two men – I push him away, just lightly, but it hurts him. I can tell, even turning my back to him – it hurts him.

He doesn't say anything. Neither of us does. Even here, even now, wrapped in the cocoon of this Blackjack home, this interim moment shared within the walls of a manor with a view of the manmade lake below, I can't be *like that* with *him*. I can't allow myself to be that way. I can't let myself *enjoy* being with another *man*, no matter how much we've changed, how far we are now from being human.

In the silence, my eyes drift through the dusty light, drift across the broken bed frame, the bookcase and the dresser wedged against the door. I try not to think about yesterday, about what happened, just dismiss it instead. Maybe I'm still in shock. Don't know. Stoff reaches over, starts to knead my shoulder again and I close my eyes.

Long walk to Cinder Hill still ahead of us. Hot day still ahead of us. After a few minutes, I stir, sit up. Stoff's hand falls away, rests flat and open on the mattress beside me. We stay like that for a moment. Neither of us speaks, but we both rise at the same time, both work together to clear the door. When we cross back into the house, we startle a family of raccoons, watch them as they amble into the sagging darkness of a downstairs bathroom. The floor is all moldy carpet, originally orange, maybe brown or red, now covered with white chips of broken plaster. A suitcase rests by the door as if waiting for someone to pick it up, take it into a world still full of neon and fast food, men with porkpie hats and women with flowery dresses.

On the whole, the house looks relatively untouched. No evidence of anyone but the raccoons using it as a nest. No graffiti or trash on the floor. Stoff and I turn out the cabinets, find a reusable grocery sack in the pantry and stuff it with anything canned that looks like it might still be edible. Most of what might have been left behind by the original owners was dry goods – pasta, rice, boxes and sacks, stuff that rats tore into years ago. Only shreds of cardboard remain now, dusty, full of rat shit.

There's about half a gallon of water in the fridge. One of those old plastic milk jug things. Everything around it is black, hard, was probably all fruit, cheese, that kind of stuff. Stoff cleans up the outside of the jug with a rag, elects to carry it.

We share a cold breakfast of canned beans on acorn bread, eat it while sitting on opposite kitchen counters, facing each other. Something about the house almost seems to insulate us from what we both know is ahead. The heat, the road, the reality of arriving in Cinder Hill without Hima, without salvage, with only bad news for a disorganized community. A new gang on the roads. A new threat to watch out for. Driverless cars and airplanes. Just thinking about all of it makes my head hurt.

"No one's going to believe us," Stoff says, almost as if he can read my mind.

"About what happened?"

"Yeah."

I nod. It's all I can think of to do, the only response that makes sense. A nod before I look away, close my eyes.

"Whole thing is fucked up," Stoff eventually adds, shakes his head.

We spend the rest of the meal in silence, eat slow. It's nearing noon by the time we finally shoulder our meager supplies, hit the steep road that leads up out of Blackjack and back to the canyonside stretch of Oborn Ferry. The heat, the incline – by the time we reach the main road, we're out of breath, sweating. I glance back at the reservoir far below, linger on the curb of the road, grimace. The water looks good, looks cool and inviting. I almost suggest a swim to Stoff, but quickly put the thought out of my head. We're still in the middle of nowhere, still in danger of running into gangs, *that gang* or others. We've still got a dozen miles or so of walking ahead of us, and only until sundown to reach the Sunday market, warn those planning on leaving about the men, the hara, the gang that hit us on the road.

My resolve doesn't stick. It lasts only about as long as it takes Oborn Ferry to wander down to the bridge at the bottom of the canyon, just a mile and change from Blackjack. The water in the reservoir is high, comes up onto the road in places, and I can't help but grin when Stoff stops, sets the twenty-two in a dry patch of gravel, pulls off his shirt, tosses aside his jeans and walks out into the water.

Doesn't take me long to follow his example, ditch my own shirt. Something in the movements, the way he splashes water against his face, scrubs at his dirty hair with strong, sinuous fingers erodes my drive to push on. Pulling off my own pants, I watch as he drops below the surface of the reservoir, rises again, breathes a loud, grateful exhale to the canyon walls.

The water in the reservoir is cold, far colder than the water in the sea of the Valley-That-Was. It's all meltwater, run-off from the heat of summer hitting the snowpacks on the cold peaks of the mountains to the east. I shiver as I wade in, stop when I'm up to my waist. Stoff is facing away from me, and as I watch him dip, rise again, my eyes are drawn to the bruises rippling across his back, swathes of blue on black, the red scouring of road rash.

All reminders of the day before. All reminders of the road ahead.

I try to put it out of my head. Again, I feel almost insulated by the walls of the canyon, the cool emptiness of the reservoir, the knowledge that there's still food in Blackjack, probably. Stoff looks at me across the water, tries a smile, but it doesn't stick. Without Hima to push us, without the weight of the others to carry us along like leaves on a tide, we're almost lost. Almost. I close my eyes, squeeze them against the thoughts, against wants, needs, illusions. I slam my face into the water, then force myself back to the surface, exhale hard, loud. Water runs down from my hair, but I brush it aside with both hands, fling it back into the reservoir. *That much,* I tell myself. *No more.*

I can feel Stoff watching me as I wade back to shore,

but I don't turn. I force myself to ignore him instead. No matter how much I might want to, I know we can't stay out here, can't go feral and expect to survive. We have to make it to Cinder Hill before nightfall. We have to do the right thing, the *human* thing. We have to do what Hima would have wanted us to do, what he would have done if he'd have survived instead of me, instead of Stoff.

"I bet the fishing here is good," Stoff says suddenly, but I ignore him, ignore the frustration in his voice. I pull my clothes back on, gather up the rifle, the snatch of food and water. Turning back toward Blackjack, Stoff gestures futilely. He knows where I stand. I can see it in the way he wades toward the shore, hedging his bets, not wanting to get left behind. "Some nice houses back there," he says, "We could fix one of them up, live good. . ."

I don't say anything. What can I say? He's right. I know he's right and – worse - I share his illusion, his vision for how life *could* be. I close my eyes, shake my head, shove aside the tantalizing images of shoreside barbeques, of hot days, cold nights with Stoff, with my drinking buddy, with the warmth, the tenderness –

"Tyse," he calls out as I push ahead, start for the bridge. "Tyse, wait!"

Splashes as he hurries toward the shore. I don't wait. I'm halfway across the bridge when he finally catches up to me, shoes squeaking with water. I hand him the rifle without looking at him and he doesn't say anything else. I know that my eyes are hard, dark with resolve. It's a battle, leaving the canyon. A silent battle, waged entirely within me, but with every step, I can feel my human side winning. There might have been a future for us in Blackjack if we'd stayed, but I can't see it. I can't see anything beyond the crumbling houses, the gangs, the coyotes, the mountain lions, all manner of threats that could sweep down in the day or night and slaughter one or both of us without warning. I can't see anything but eventually letting down the walls between me and Stoff, admitting my feelings for *another man,* and that –

I close my eyes. I can see a future in Cinder Hill. I can see a future where Stoff and I might manage to gather some guys to round out a new salvage team. I can see a future full of Sunday markets and dives from the side of the trawler into the sea of the Valley-That-Was. I can see life being normal again, as close to normal as it ever was, but there's no room in that future for a life together in the canyon, in Blackjack. There's no room in that future for what we both want, only what we have to do.

"Gotta pick up the pace if we're going to make the market in time," I say, let the words hang quiet in the air.

Stoff sighs, looks ahead, doesn't say anything more.

CHAPTER 9

There's a reason why they call the hills out here the *Gold Country*. It isn't just because of the mines, the greed-hollowed hills, the history. In the summer, in the warm months when all the grass dries up and dies, everything is literally *gold*. It's beautiful, but it's also hot as shit. Triple-digits usually this time of year. The heat coming up from the road is killer, makes it worse.

The chill of the meltwater evaporating from our skin makes the long hike back up the other side of the canyon a little less hellish, but it doesn't last long. By the time we're halfway up the twisting road, we're dry, taking swigs from what's left of the water in the jug we found in Blackjack. Mentally, I forecast our route, the route we'd be taking if we still had the trucks – eventually, Oborn Ferry dumps into the Eighty Eight. It's not much of a highway, two lanes and that's it, but it makes for fast cruising over dry country, pushes straight into the center of Cinder Hill.

That's not the route we take, though. The road is too hot, wanders enough to add a couple of miles to our walk if we were to follow it. There are also houses and a prison we'd pass if we stuck to the pavement. Not sure if anyone lives in any of them, but, if anyone does, a pair of thirsty hara are certainly a more inviting target than a pair of speeding trucks. Last thing Stoff or I want is to end up as anyone's dinner, or worse.

As soon as we reach the top of the canyon, we cast a last glance back at the reservoir, take our reading from the sun. When we break from the road, we head north-east toward the lowest-lying point of a great flat length of long, sheer-sided mountain. Even after years of neglect, most of the barbed wire fences between us and the mountain still stand, but we're both thin enough to duck and slip between the lines. To make it easier, we hold the wires for each other, pull one and push the other with a foot to force more room.

Even wading through the waist-high fields of dead grass, we make good time. By some miracle, neither of us startles or steps on a rattlesnake. Jeans and bare feet in beat-up shoes keep most of the stickers we knock loose from hitching a ride on our clothing, but we still get nicks here and there from the sharp yellow spines of star thistle heads hidden in the grass. Eventually, we spot a fire road from the crest of a low rise, hook up with it and follow it over the lowest point of the flat mountain.

Dry grass gives way to dust, to gravel. There's more star thistle where the grass thins, but at least it's easier to spot, easier to avoid. The fire road follows the curve of a dirt hill, cuts north across the dead, basalt surface of the flat mountain. Easy hike – the incline isn't too bad here. Other parts of the long, flat mountain stick up higher, hundreds of feet, make for almost impassible terrain, but there are breaks in the flow, places where the whole thing dips into the dirt, almost disappears from view.

As soon as we cross, we start almost directly east again, keep the length of the mountain on our right. As far as landmarks go, the mountain is perfect – always there, unusual in appearance, easy to follow. It's the only remnant of the bottom of an ancient river canyon obliterated tens of millions of years ago by a flow of lava from the mountains to the east. The land around it is different now, so different than it was then. Even while erosion has cut down the hills that once towered over the

70

river, the basalt cast of the ancient canyon still remains, stands as a mountain now, slithering across the tree-spotted countryside like a massive, black and rough-skinned snake.

Doesn't take long before we're back in the grass again, pushing our way over ground flattened by a century or so of grazing cattle. *Better times* – the only trace of livestock we see as we walk are bones scattered in the dirt here and there. A vertebra, a piece of sun-dried leather with a tuft of hair still stuck to it. No skulls. No chunks of bone bigger than a fist. All that stuff was broken up and picked clean long ago.

Four miles cross-country and we hit the edge of another reservoir. Dusty and tired, we don't bother to take our clothes off, just wade into the waves and track along the muddy shore there until Stoff spots the pitted pavement of Shell Road curving in from the north. Reluctantly, we leave the water, cross the flood-plains beyond the reach of the reservoir, slip through another barbed-wire fence and cut across a few dozen feet of gravel lot. Shell isn't big, but it's easy to follow, connects up with the larger roads that we know will eventually meet the Eighty-Eight just outside of Cinder Hill. My feet are tired, aching. We're both sunburnt and sore, but still we push on. "Only a few miles to go," I breathe, but Stoff doesn't respond. The sun is halfway to the horizon. I give him the last mouthful from the jug, close my eyes as he empties it, tosses it into the weeds. *Plenty of water in Cinder Hill,* I tell myself. *Just a few more miles.*

Houses rise up out of the weeds as the trees get thicker. The edges of little suburbs, little planned neighborhoods built a half century or so before everything fell apart, stick out between stands of live oak and ponderosa pine, cluster in larger and larger knots the closer we get to Cinder Hill. Most of the houses are empty, fire-blackened and open to the sun, but here and there little signs of life stand out among the ruins. A garden, heavily fenced to keep out the deer, the rabbits and the thieves on two legs. A well shaded from the sun with a tarp weighed down by old tires and rocks. A shining oil spot on concrete where a truck was parked until just this morning, until the Sunday market, when it would be used to bring food, booze, salvage or any number of other things out for trade on the streets of Cinder Hill. One big tailgate sale, that's what the market is. That's where almost everyone is on Sunday, even during the hottest part of the summer.

We're limping, moving slow by the time we catch the rising length of South Washington. There isn't much shade, but we stick to it where we find it, stay with the road and the curb as much as we can to make up for time lost to fatigue and to cooling ourselves where we could.

The last few golden hills pass, and then the road levels out. The post office is the first building that comes in sight, or rather the building that was the post office. It's someone's home now, the wide, wrap-around parking lot strewn with piles of rusting junk. A dog spots us from the shade under the overhang, starts barking, stays with her litter of brown and white, pit-mix puppies instead of coming after us. Stoff glances at the dog, watches her for a moment as she pauses, holds herself at the edge of a bark, then growls as he looks away again. In moments, she's behind us, silent, forgotten.

The last quarter mile before the Sunday market feels like the longest leg of the journey. So many buildings I recognize, so many landmarks that would be roaring by if we were in a car or a truck. Here and there, hara look up, notice us, say nothing. We're in bad shape, beat to shit and dead on our feet, but that's not an unusual look for folk who wander into Cinder Hill on foot. Nobody recognizes us at a distance. Nobody stops us or offers to help us. No reason they should. Hima they might know on sight, but not us. Neither of us has ever brokered any trades on Hima's behalf. We've always been just a couple of nameless Joes doing the grunt work behind the scenes. Nothing special. No one worth remembering, least not by these folks.

Further in, though, that's sure to change.

The three or six blocks of main street Cinder Hill on either side of the intersection at the center of town are alive with movement when we arrive. Pickup trucks piled high with summer crops, fruit, all manner of junk and luxuries crowd the street like stalls, some covered with tarp-tents braced by aging lengths of PVC pipe. From every tailgate, hatchback and trailer, folks shout their wares, but the shouts come half-hearted now, dulled by the day, by the heat. Some of the voices I recognize, most of them I don't. It's late enough that some are already packing their goods away for the day. We don't have much time. Some of them will be hitting the road soon, headed for points north, points west, points out along the Four, out along Oborn Ferry. They have to know what's out there, what we ran into.

I push myself harder, force my feet into a stumbling trot. In the middle of the knot of vendors sits the town's old hotel, the Cinder Hill Inn – that's where we need to go, Stoff and I. A drink, if we can barter for it with what we have, and the ear of one of the most powerful men in Cinder Hill. Bill Hastings, the closest thing the town has to a mayor or a governor, and a close personal friend of Captain Hima. Like some rough relic of the gold rush days that still cling so close in the minds and memories of all the guys who grew up steeped in the cowboy mystique of Cinder Hill's tourist-trap facade, Bill has always been a rock, an anchor of the old world we could rally to.

Books, dried meat, hand-reloaded bullets, wildflower wine – the shouts mingle and thicken as we descend into the eye of the Sunday chaos. A few folks look up as we hurry by, watch us with worried or wary eyes. To warn them now, to start shouting in the streets – it wouldn't do much good. We need clout, we need volume. We need a voice that can reach everyone and be trusted by them all. We need Hastings, and his name is the first one I yell the instant I shove my way through the swinging, age-beaten double-doors of the Cinder Hill Inn.

"Bill! Somebody get me Bill!" A couple of hara look up from the bar just inside, stare at me, at Stoff. Most are dressed as we are – dirty jeans, shirts faded and full of little tears, little holes from getting caught on bolts or nails. It's like a uniform among the Thuulhuum of the hollow hills, marks them all as locals. The bartender takes one look at us, doesn't even waste time nodding. He sets down the glass and rag in his hands, immediately crosses through the swinging door between the bar and the kitchen. In the sudden silence, one of the guys at the bar shifts a wad of tobacco in his mouth, chews it for a moment, then spits a wet chunk into the sawdust covering the floor.

Stoff looks at me. I take a moment to catch my breath, to shift my weight to the sides of my feet in an attempt to take some of the pressure off the blisters on my soles and heels. Hastings pushes his way through the kitchen door, takes one look at us over a pair of gold-rimmed glasses, then makes a sharp gesture with a thumb, indicating a table further in.

I glance at the bartender as he returns to the bar, give a nod and get one back in response. Hastings pulls out chairs for Stoff and I even before we reach the table, gestures for us to sit with big, meaty hands.

"Where's Hima?" is the first thing he asks.

"Dead," Stoff says, puts the word out there before I can even start to speak. Bill cocks an eyebrow, regards Stoff carefully through the pair of delicate-looking spectacles. I swallow in the pause, take a breath, and then Bill's eyes are on me and all I can think about is how silly it is that he still wears those glasses. He might have needed them once, but now that he's har, they're just an affectation, just costume jewelry worn by a grown man still bigger and more full of muscle than most. Hell, I know the guy who replaced the original prescription lenses with clear glass –

"Tyse," Bill cuts the thought in half. "What happened?"

"There's a new gang–" I falter, unable to finish. "Something like a gang." I swallow, force myself to continue. "We saw some weird shit out there on Oborn Ferry, out by the Goodwin Reservoir, maybe a mile or two out of Blackjack on the Copperburg side."

"Define *weird shit,*" he says, his eyes never leaving mine.

"Well like, there was this car," Stoff says quickly, swallows nervously as Bill's eyes slide to lock with his. "It um – it came right up on us from the Blackjack side of Oborn Ferry not long after we'd pulled through

Copperburg." He pauses, shakes his head. "It tried to ram us, Bill. I swear to god, it tried to ram us, merged right into our lane and clipped Hima's truck. Musta been going sixty or seventy–"

"But that wasn't the weird part," I put in suddenly. Stoff looks at me, licks his lips apprehensively, looks back at Bill as I continue. "This car – it didn't have a driver. It came right up on us, chased us, hit both trucks multiple times, *all without a driver.*"

"Bullshit," Bill says, just puts the word out there, but I can tell from his tone he's not entirely convinced yet that we're batshit crazy. *Work with it.* I swallow, steel myself.

"It's true!" Stoff puts in. "We were both there. We were riding with Yuri. I saw Ray and Tyse both put rounds in the driver's seat of that car and the thing didn't even *flinch.*"

"Yuri managed to spin it off the road when it got between our truck and Hima's, but even after it hit a tree, you could tell it was still trying to get loose." I nod. "Nobody got out, nobody shot at us–"

"And there was this airplane," Stoff nods, glances at me. "Not like the ones out at the county airport, not like the civilian beer-can-with-wings birds they have on the tarmac out there. This thing was *black,* sleek." He glances at me again.

"Military, probably," I finish, eyes never leaving Bill's.

"So how'd Hima die?" Bill asks.

Stoff and I look at each other. Neither of us saw the impact, the exact moment when everything went to hell. Neither of us really thought about getting our story together, about how we'd explain the one part of the story that's the most important. I swallow, meet Bill's eyes again.

"I – he hit. . ." I struggle with the words, breathe, considering. "Something happened. After the plane, after the car, there were these four guys on the road. They walked right out into the road and Hima made clear he was going to run them down if they didn't get out of the way. Stoff and I got down, braced ourselves, and then–" I shake my head, unsure of how to proceed. Everything that comes after that moment is a blur, disjointed frames that make about as much sense as an old Lynch film. I frown, trying to remember, but the only image that sticks out is that chunk of steel from Hima's truck sailing overhead. *The hood,* I realize. *Jesus, it was the hood.*

"Tyse!" The sharpness in Bill's tone brings me back. My eyes rise, meet his. "What happened? There were men on the road. Humans? Hara? Varr? Uigenna?"

"I don't know who they were, what they were, Bill." I swallow, hesitate for a moment. "I only saw one of them up close, and he was wearing a mask. Black glass, the whole thing, like some kind of freaky spacesuit. He mighta been an alien for all I know, Bill. He moved weird. He did things – I saw him kill Davy with a single punch, and then he picked up one of our twenty-twos and he just. . . he broke it into little pieces with his bare hands."

Bill looks at me carefully, considering. "You've got some pretty serious bruises there, Tyse," he says. "You sure you didn't just bump your head and–"

"It's true," Stoff cuts him off, earns a sharp, studying stare. "I saw Davy. I saw the gun. Both trucks were thrashed. Hima was literally crushed to death in the cab of his." He pauses, licks his lips. "They tore us apart, Bill. Just four of them. They stopped us dead from a run. Hima had to be going at least sixty, and when they were done with us, there weren't nothing but little chunks of metal and glass left. It's strewn all over the road up there. You can see it yourself, if you take a truck out before dusk."

"Might do, tomorrow." Bill nods, looks at me again. "What'd they take? Food? The usual? They leave in trucks? Bikes? Horseback?"

"They left on foot," I say. Can't blame Bill for the look he gives me. "No vehicles but the one Yuri knocked off the road, and they only took one thing."

"The rock," Stoff says quickly, glancing at me. It's as much a question as it is a statement. I nod in response.

"The rock," I confirm. "A meteorite we found near Stock Town. Thing probably weighs a thousand pounds or more. They knew exactly where it was, and it was all they took."

"Friggin' space aliens," Stoff says, shakes his head. "Gotta be friggin' space aliens."

Bill looks at Stoff for a moment, then meets my eyes again. In the pause, he breathes a tired sigh, finally stands, glances back at the bar, gestures to the bartender.

"I can't stop those who've already left, but you're here early enough that I can get the word out to most of the folks who've come for the market. I'll have a couple of my boys pass the warning around to avoid Oborn Ferry until I can get some people up there to check it out, verify your story." He turns immediately to the bartender as the guy stops beside him. "Get these two a room and something to eat. Leftovers, whatever." He gestures at us. "Make sure they don't go anywhere until I say otherwise." He looks at me, extends a hand. "I'll take your gun."

I don't fight him on it, don't argue. I understand where he's coming from, how this whole mess must look to him. I unsling the twenty-two, pass it to him immediately, knowing I'll get it back someday, maybe. Depends on how big a tab we rack up eating leftovers in one of Bill's rooms while we wait. Bill throws the strap over his own shoulder, offers us a gruff, momentary smile as the bartender gestures, indicates a staircase beyond the bar with a polite: "gentlemen."

"Be careful out there, Bill," I offer, standing for a moment before crossing to follow Stoff and the other har to the stairs. Bill only looks at me, his eyes wary, tired. Eventually he nods, pulls in a deep breath.

"Yeah," is all he says before he turns, crosses out of the Inn and into the street beyond.

CHAPTER 10

Sunday night. As the sun sets, Stoff and I sit by the creaky, slow-turning fan braced in the open frame of our room's only window. Beyond the sill, the lights across the street and around The Mall flare to life with the cough and sputter of an old generator retrofitted with cannibalized parts that allow it to run by burning a steady supply of firewood. Black smoke rises into the air behind the old three story brick building, and we watch as the crowd in the streets separates, divides, most of the hara there packing up their wares or purchases and heading off home. The few who stay are locals and tourists; I spot a knot of Uigenna kids in their torn-up punk gear, note their leader's swagger, his thick, bright-orange mohawk spilling off his scalp where it doesn't spike. I note the patches on his faded vest – northern kids, probably. Not from as far north as Duwamish, not from The Rift, probably some place in between. One of his thugs glances up, notices me and Stoff, makes a gesture with his fist that's half *rock on* and half *fuck you* before they laugh, cross into The Mall with the rest of the night crowd trickling in from the streets.

There's a knock at the door and I look up lazily. No need to get up – it's a courtesy knock. We're locked in, couldn't let anyone in if we wanted to.

Three guys are at the door when it opens, two of them trustworthy locals who Bill is paying to make sure we don't leave. The other guy is some low-man-on-the-totem-pole from the kitchen, and he offers a quick smile as he collects the plates from our meal of scraps and leftovers, tops off our carafe of room-temperature water. Even before he leaves, my eyes are back on the street below, wandering amongst the hara down there, picking out details in the failing light. Stoff watches the peon until he leaves, nods to the guard who closes the door. The guard smiles back – he's seen us, he knows we're no threat, that we're not waiting for a chance to escape. We'd be dead if we were any threat to anyone. This whole *locked in a room with guards* bullshit is just a job to him. For Bill, it's standard procedure whenever a raid survivor wanders into town with a fishy story to tell about how he escaped. Allows Bill to keep an eye on the guy or guys in question, allows him to make sure they haven't gone *feral*, that they aren't going to betray the first caravan they ride out with.

"What do you think?" I make a quick gesture, point out a pair of guys with their hands on each others' asses. One's wearing something like a skirt, the other's got on way too much jewelry. Both look out of place amongst the locals. "Unneah?"

Stoff looks at the two guys, hesitates for a minute, watches them until they wander into The Mall. "Nah, not Unneah."

"They don't dress like any of the Varrs I've seen or heard of," I offer.

"Might be from one of them southern tribes." Stoff chews his lip a little. "I hear some of them like to run around in dresses."

"They aren't usually that fruity though, right?"

"I dunno," Stoff says, leaves it at that. I look over at him, watch him as he watches the people in the street. Shadows mingle with the mud and the sunburn on his face, and for a moment I let my eyes linger on him, on the mix of fatigue and sadness pulling at his lips, his eyes. When he finally looks up, he meets my eyes evenly, and a little of that sadness seems to fall away. "Whatcha looking at?"

His tone is friendly, but I look away anyway. "Nothing," I say, careful not to let loose any of the words I want to say, the words in my chest that are making me uncomfortable. Taking a deep breath, I stomp the feelings down, wonder if Stoff is doing the same. Crazy times we live in.

"I was thinking, you know Nicky over up on Bald Mountain Lane?" Stoff breaks the silence, scratches at his dirt-stiffened hair. "When Bill lets us out, we might go talk to him. He's strong. Last thing I heard, he was looking for steady work. Might make a good diver for when we take the trawler out again."

"We're going to need trucks first," I say, words coming quiet, distant. After a minute, I look back, meet his eyes again. "We're going to need some way to haul salvage from the trawler to the market."

"We could get horses," Stoff says. "Horses are cheap."

"Can't take horses apart and put them back together again like you can a truck," I shake my head. "Can't leave them at our tie-up point and expect them to be there after we've been gone a week." I look down, breathe, look back. "Besides, we'd need a whole pack of them to carry a load heavy enough to be worth the trouble. No, it's gotta be trucks with trailers or nothing."

Stoff's eyes wander back to the fan in the silence that follows. The sadness is back in his features, and I can't blame him for it. The more I think about the future now, the more hosed I realize we probably are. Hima had a lot of infrastructure tied up in his operation, infrastructure we don't have, can't get easy or cheap. Hell, even the trawler'll be useless to us unless we can get fuel, batteries, a smattering of tools and a dozen other things out to it. All we really have to our name right now is the food in our bellies, the gun that'll probably be taken to pay for it and the temporary kindness of near-strangers. Isn't much. Doesn't give me much hope.

"Should've stayed in Blackjack," Stoff says then, his quiet words echoing my thoughts. I can't look at him after he says it, can't speak. In my heart, I know that he's probably right. I hate it, but I know that he's probably right.

Minutes pass with only the noise of the night. A pair of guys wander out of The Mall, get caught up in each other's arms, stumble into the doorway of a building in a tangle of hands, legs and sliding clothes. When they start to fuck right there on the street, I look away, swallow against the feelings their noises fire within me. Stoff swallows too. I can smell his sweat.

"Someone had to tell Bill about the gang we ran into," I say, but the words come weak, ring hollow. Stoff looks at me again then, and in the brief moment I meet his eyes, I can see that he knows exactly how I feel, exactly what I'm thinking, what feelings I'm hiding. When he reaches out, touches me, touches one leg so tenderly, I shiver. I can't help it, and he reads me so easily.

The guys in the street are yowling like feral cats when we kiss, when our lips meet, part again, tremble so close, so close, wet and eager for more. It hurts, but it's also so sweet, so necessary. There's sound, like a wave rising, crashing, and I know that there's no going back now. I feel one of his hands as it touches my face, and then I reach out, find my hand on the curve of his side, his hip. I can't bear to look at him, close my eyes instead and let other images come to me, images of women, of a woman who Stoff vaguely reminds me of. The kiss picks up, becomes rougher, more passionate, and then I'm tearing his shirt off, reaching for his chest, squeezing, pinching nipples while I think about breasts, about big, juicy breasts and curvy thighs, about the hairy cleft I want, I *need* to feel wrapped around me.

It doesn't go the way I want it to. Stoff pushes me onto my back mid-kiss, shoves me to the bed and presses me hard into the musty sheets. Instantly, I can feel my dick-thing opening, turning inward, moistening, *hungry*, but in my mind, passions and memories and fantasies battle like angry dogs in a pit fight. I want him, but I don't want *him*. I want the girl I knew when I was human, the girl he reminds me of, sort of. The girl who had the same eyes, similar hair – the girl I fucked behind the bleachers a couple of times during our last week as seniors at the local high school. Just thinking about her, about my hard cock sliding into her hot, hairy little muff gets my hips bucking, and that throws Stoff off, slows him a little. I reach up, touch his face, realize his eyes are closed too, realize that we're both fucking a fantasy, both lusting after women who don't exist anymore, who died a long time ago.

Something about the thought, the realization puts me off enough that I stop kissing Stoff, turn my head to the side. Already, I can feel myself closing off to him, can feel the flame within me fading, frustrated and unsatisfied. Stoff's hips move a little more, slow as his body responds to mine, to my sudden flaccidity, my lack of passion and need. Half-mast, pants wadded up around his ankles, Stoff eventually pushes himself off me, flops over onto the bed beside me, tries to catch his breath.

"Dammit," is all he can say.

I agree, don't voice it. My eyes open, and for a moment I just lie there listening, staring at the ceiling. The hara in the street have gone silent, finished up and moved on to other things. In the distance, someone laughs and I get up, cross to the table by the door, pour myself a glass of water, pull my pants back on, button them without looking over at Stoff.

There are a thousand things I want to say, a thousand things I *should* say, but I give breath to none of them. Half of the sentences rushing through my brain are half-formed, half-considered. There are things I need, things that make sense, things that don't. I turn, look at Stoff, look at the way he's sprawled on the bed, pants still wrapped around one ankle, the other hanging free, his dick-thing slowly retracting, softening, almost like a flower drawing back its petals, returning to the shape of a bud. His chest glistens with sweat, hairless, like the chest of a woman with bee-stings instead of hefty bags. I hate to admit it, won't voice it, but he *turns me on.* Stoff. *Something about Stoff really does turn me on.*

"What does God want us to do, Stoff?" The words come out before I can stop them, tired and full of restrained need. I hate it immediately – it isn't what I want to know, what I care about, what frustrates me. I can't put the real thoughts into words. I can't push into the light what I really want to ask him. Blinking, still breathing heavily, he props himself up on his elbows, looks at me for a long, quiet moment. Only when I look away, force myself to take a drink from the glass of water does he answer.

"You mean..." he manages, lets the sentence trail off.

In the pause, I look back at him, meet his eyes. "This," I gesture at myself, at him, at the world. I can't voice everything I feel – there aren't enough words in the world to express my frustration, my thoughts, the things I want, the things I need. "There're no more women. No one's seen one in forever. There's just *us*, guys like us." I shake my head. "Just a lot of horny guys with *those–*" I gesture at his crotch. "Those mutated *dick-things* that open up, get all wet like pussies." I meet his eyes, can see the pain there, the fire, the same emotions battling across his face. "Does God want us all to be a bunch of faggots? Are we supposed to all just fuck each other and get married? One of us start wearing dresses, start cooking and dusting and shit while the other goes off to work at the fucking mine or the mill?"

"Jesus, Tyse," he breathes, and it's then that I realize I'm crying, that tears are budding at the edges of my eyes. It makes me mad, *real mad*. My hands clench into fists, but I keep them in check. If the yelling doesn't bring the guys outside the door to check on us, breaking something *will*.

"I don't know what God wants, Tyse." Stoff says. I look at him in the pause, meet his eyes evenly. "I don't know that anyone does. I've never read the Bible, haven't been to church since I was five. Doesn't matter. I do what feels right in the moment. I do what I believe is right, and if God made us this way, made us feel the way we do, well. . ." He shakes his head, lets the words trail off. I feel the sting of new tears fighting to get out and I sniff, rub at my eyes, hate how childlike it must look.

"You fucked Hima, right?" Stoff asks after a moment, waits for me to look at him again. "Davy too?"

I could lie. I feel like I should lie, but I don't. "Yeah," I manage, leave it at that.

"Did it feel good?" He licks his lips apprehensively, hesitates.

"I was thinking about one of my old girlfriends both times," I say, deflecting the question.

"So was I," Stoff says, and there's a quaver in the steely confidence he's trying to keep up. "Both times I was with Davy, all five times I fucked Hima, but not the *whole time.*"

I pause, consider his words. I want to ask him what he means, already know *exactly* what he means.

"Tyse," he tries, and my eyes rise to lock with his again. "I never was a faggot. Dick and man-ass never got me hard, but we aren't men anymore, are we? We're something different now. We're something *more.*"

I can't argue with him. I know he's right. I look away on reflex and, thinking he's lost me, Stoff adds: "You turn me on, Tyse. *You* do."

I look up again. I remember touching his face, finding closed eyes with searching fingers. The words come out before I can stop them, before I can think about how they sound.

"You were thinking about someone else," I hesitate, gesture. "Just now."

"Yeah, a little," he admits. "This," he gestures at the air between us. "It's as new and weird for me as it is for you. I'm not over pussy either, you know? I still wish I had a girl with a nice, big pair of tits to play with, but there's something about us, about *hara* that kinda turns me on even more than the curviest woman I can imagine would, something that my body craves more than cigarettes and good whiskey."

I say nothing. I know what he means. I feel the heat of it, the echo of his words like an ember burning in the very heart of me. Turning fully to face him, I look at him, really look at him for what feels like the first time. Sweat runs down his chest. His autumn eyes rise under dark hair, even with mine.

"I turn you on too," he says, and there's no guile to his words, no smile, no tease. It's a statement, an observation. He's right – again, I know he's right, but something about committing myself fully to that path, that side of *me* seems wrong, seems like a betrayal of all that I am, all that I was. The world is changing so fast even still, even after the chaos that tore the old world apart calmed and seemed to pass.

It never passed though, not really. It never got better, and any sense of things returning to the way they were was just illusion. Ten years ago, twenty, however long ago it was that I lived in Cinder Hill as a man, as a human, any man who laid down with another man as he might otherwise with a woman would have been driven out of town, and only that if he was lucky. He would have been called all manner of horrible names, would have been stalked by guys with tire-irons in their hands and beer on their breath, beaten and sodomized with shovel handles until he bled. The nurses and doctors would turn their backs on him if he sought their help. The courts, the police, they'd do the same. He'd have no choice but to leave, head west, head to the coast, where there were more like him and fewer like the "good Christian folk" of Cinder Hill.

"I can't, Stoff," I finally breathe, and I hate myself for it. My mind is a mass of conflicting concepts, ideas of right and wrong, and how what seemed right or wrong, might actually be the opposite if looked at in another light. Why is it wrong for a man to want to fuck another man? Way I was taught, it was all about the Bible, the Word of God. All faggots were sinners, and sinners go to hell. Never really believed too much in heaven or hell myself, but maybe – and even just thinking about *that whole mess* scares the shit out of me, opens a whole new can of worms–

"You want to," Stoff says, cutting the thought short. I can hear the way his resolve cracks a little as the words leave his lips. He wants it. He wants me, but I – to do it, to like it, to admit that, allow myself to accept Stoff as more than just a drinking buddy, as someone I'm intimate with, a man who's as interested in fucking me as I am him – *Jesus!*

"It's–" I swallow, shake my head. "It's a lot, Stoff. It's more than. . ." I sigh, trying to get the words out, slam my hand against the table in frustration. *Say it.* "Yes, I want to fuck you. Yes, you turn me on, but I–" The words get caught in my throat, take a moment to work loose. "Stoff, our friendship is the last piece of the way things were that I have left. If I lose that, if I lose my drinking buddy, my... my *man-ness*, whatever you call it – I –"

I stop, can't finish the sentence. Somewhere on the street below, a pair of guys shout something at one another and it softens the moment, brings us both back to the room, the world, the balmy night. Stoff gets up off the bed, crosses to me, glistening and naked, puts one hand on my shoulder. I close my eyes. I want to hurt him, beat him straight, but I also want what he wants. I want peace. I want *this*.

"It's scary, I know," he says, voice coming soft.

"I ain't afraid of nothing," I say quickly, gritting teeth against more fucking tears.

"It's like a lake, Tyse," Stoff whispers, reaches up,

caresses the back of my neck, runs his fingers into my hair. I shiver, can't speak. "You can't just dive in and hope you learn to swim. You have to start where it's shallow, wade in, *feel the water.*"

Lips peel back from my teeth. It takes every ounce of resolve I have not to bust out bawling like a baby. Stoff holds me close, kisses my cheek the way a woman might.

"What was her name?" he asks.

"Who?" I choke out the question, regret the pain that comes so strong in my voice.

"The woman you were thinking of a little bit ago."

I swallow again, think back. Dark hair, same green-brown, autumn-colored eyes as Stoff, almost the same short, dark hair. Great tits, curvy ass–

"Louise," I burble. *Jesus.*

"Louise," he echoes, kisses my shoulder, works his way down my chest. "You can pretend I'm Louise, Tyse. I want you to pretend I'm Louise."

I open my eyes, reach out for him. "Stoff."

He stops me, looks up at me. "Close your eyes. Call me Louise. Make love to Louise, Tyse. Just – just be with Louise for a little while."

And then his tongue is on my dick-thing, teasing it, taking it into his mouth so gently. I close my eyes as the pleasure moves through me, and soon, soon I'm with Louise, I'm back on the football field with Louise, sneaking behind the bleachers between classes, watching her as she goes to work on me, as she sucks me until I'm raring like a stallion, eager and hungry, pushing her back, mounting her while she grins, while she laughs.

And just before I cum, just before I let myself go, I open my eyes, find *him* there. The orgasm rolls through me, rises into him like a wave, and in that moment, in that moment when I become one with him, I realize I don't want to be anywhere else. I don't want to be *with* anyone else. I want him. Just him.

"*Stoff,*" I whisper his name and I see him grin like a sonofabitch as I shudder into him, tense, then fall into the sheets, half-dead, utterly spent.

CHAPTER 11

Dawn comes, and with it the sound of a normal Monday morning in the center of Cinder Hill. I wipe the crust of saliva from my lips, realize I've hardly moved since last night, since Stoff and I–

I blink, push over onto my side. Stoff's got his back to me, his breath coming slow, even. In the distance, I can hear chickens, the hungry grumble of a goat. The Mall and its wood-burning generator have long since gone silent.

It isn't long before my thoughts start to wander back to the night, to *the act*. Part of me doesn't want to admit it, but I feel better, miles better than I've felt in a long time. My head's clear, nothing's numb and the thoughts that come into my mind resolve themselves easily. What we did wasn't gay, I tell myself. We aren't men, not any more. We're something else. We're doing what comes natural to us, and it's weird since we were human once, but new trails are always a little hard to blaze. Neither of us has to change, I guess. We can still be buddies. We can still be like men, dress the same, act the same way. We can still be ourselves, just, well–

We can be ourselves and still be hara, still be *what we are*, physically speaking.

That's how I rationalize it, at least. Still feels a little weird to wear it, but I know that in time, I'll get used to it. We all will. Plenty of guys have gotten used to it already. I'm nothing special, probably not even really a late bloomer. The world is weird these days. Oceans where there should be cities. Men with dicks that turn into pussies. Maybe even genuine space-aliens. No point in trying to ignore it all, trying to live in the past. Roll with the changes. It's all we really can do.

Stoff's in such a deep sleep that he doesn't even twitch when I get up, when I cross to the table by the door, fill a glass from the carafe of water. Noticing it's been refilled, probably sometime during the night, I feel momentarily embarrassed. Someone came in at some point, may have seen something – but then, plenty of men – hara – fuck each other these days. Don't know what they were expecting to happen, putting us in a room with only one bed.

I hold the glass for a moment, watch Stoff as he sleeps. Something about it is soothing. The lines of his shoulder blades, the rising and falling of his back – it draws me in, reminds me of the night, of the *thing* we shared. From across the room, I can almost convince myself it isn't Stoff at all, that Louise is lying in my bed, freshly fucked and sleeping it off, but I don't want to. I don't want to pretend anymore. I want to be who I am, what I am.

I take a swig from the glass, push back fear as I swallow it. Stoff was right – it is scary. It is like a lake, and even now I'm not one hundred percent sure I want to learn how to swim. I know it's the right thing to do. I know that if the God my grandma believed so fervently in is real, he wouldn't have changed us like this, made us who we are, *what we are*, if he wasn't okay with us embracing it fully.

I'll just have to figure out what it means to be a man and a har as I go along.

Another slug of water and I go back to the bed. *Fuck it.* I do what feels right, caress Stoff and kiss him a couple of times, hold him as he wakes up, smiling. I feel like a woman, like a man, like both, and it doesn't matter much what Stoff is. In some ways, he's better than any girlfriend I ever had was. He's my drinking buddy, but he's also a fine piece of ass.

I reach down, caress his thigh, and as he starts to get hard, I let myself open up for him. Doesn't take long before I'm on my back, grinning, feeling that strange, feminine side of myself, sinking into it, somehow still feeling male without feeling like anything's too weird or wrong. He shivers as he slides into me, grins wide as we start to move together. This time, I don't think about Louise. I don't think about any woman. I let myself be turned on by Stoff. I let myself be fully honest with my body for what feels like the first time since I became har.

When we cum, it's incredible. It's as good as last night, if not a little better. Stoff trembles, exhausted, and I let him rest on my chest, hold him as he breathes raggedly into my neck. Neither one of us rests long. Something in the act, in the sharing of our bodies, in the honesty of it, the understanding is so freeing that we feel compelled to keep doing it. It feels clean, it feels *necessary,* like a good run after an age of sitting. It feels right to move together, to get the blood pumping, to cum, let fly, grind hips together and moan into mouths that nip and kiss more passionately than any woman either of us has ever been with. When I'm with him, I don't feel like a man, like a jeans and t-shirt shitkicker who spends his nights getting drunk, chasing loose tail. I feel *human* – maybe that's the wrong word. I feel *whole.* I feel completely myself, feel like something more, something beyond the simple stick man I was for so long. Stoff feels it too. I can tell. I can see it in his eyes, the way he does things, the way he follows the cues his body gives him, moves as one with me and mine. Together, we simply *are,* and it's amazing. It's wholly unlike anything I've ever experienced before.

We probably make love five times before the knock comes. Mercifully, it doesn't interrupt us, comes instead while we're resting, trying to catch our breath. A little scared, we separate before the door opens, move to opposite sides of the bed and pull up the sheets before the kitchen peon walks in, sets down a plate of leftovers from the Inn's breakfast menu. He doesn't look at us, doesn't say anything, but doesn't glare or look sick either. His movements are polite, quick but not too quick. One of the guys watching the door peeks in at us, grins, and it's a little disconcerting, but not as much as it might have been *before.* It's a sure bet that everyone who's been within a few feet of the door *knows.* The room smells like sex, and Stoff, well, he's *loud.* I'm not a whisperer either, but I don't moan half as loud when I cum as he does.

As soon as the guy from the kitchen leaves, we pounce on the plate, bring it back to the bed, share it on the sheets. Whipped cream made from goat milk, slightly sweet. Slices of Indian Free Peaches and a small pile of sun-ripened blackberries. Lightly toasted acorn bread with lemon-suffused goat butter. It's delicious, twice as much as it might have been if we weren't so utterly spent and starving from sex. As we eat, I grin at how loose I feel. Loose in a good way. Free. Totally me.

"What if we went back to Blackjack?" Stoff asks around a mouthful of cream and acorn bread. "There are still some houses out there that are set up for solar. We could live there for a while, couple of months or years, maybe, cannibalize what we can, maybe get the trawler moving again."

"Sounds real good." I nod, gesture. "Wouldn't be safe

just the two of us, though. You heard those cougars in the canyon when we were out there, right? And the coyotes? Then there's the gangs–"

"Okay, okay, I get your point." He grins. "I just – I like the idea of getting out of Cinder Hill, going somewhere else, somewhere there's more opportunity. Somewhere by the water."

"We could ask around," I offer. "See if there are any vendors that need a couple of extra hands. I know there are small communities deeper in the woods east of here. Might be one out near Cedarcrest, maybe one near the Francis-Mark Forebay."

"Those are all above the snowline. I'd like to set up somewhere warm, but near the water." He's quiet for a moment, considering. "Didn't that kid – what's his name? One we used to work with when we were shifting crates for Robert Hamilton in Jimtown?"

"Jared?" I offer. I know the guy he's talking about. Skinny with a big smile. Kind of a jack ass, but not unbearable.

"Right. Didn't Jared say that there was a group of four or five guys that went out and chained a bunch of houseboats together on New Milo Lake?"

New Milo Lake. I think about it for a moment, try to recall. I know the lake he's talking about – it's the last reservoir we slogged through to cool off yesterday during our walk back to Cinder Hill. Beautiful area – the big old table-flat mountain rising up out of the trees, the live oak and the linden always pretty and green, even when the hills are gold and dry. Lots of Indian Free Peach trees, manzanita scrub and blackberry bushes out there too. Lots to eat, and the fishing's pretty good when you get out into the deeper parts of New Milo. Can't specifically remember Jared mentioning anything about a group setting up a town out there on the water, though–

"I *think* I remember Jared saying something about it," Stoff tries, still chewing. "Maybe it was someone else."

"Bill might know," I offer. Bill knows every vendor who comes into Cinder Hill for the Sunday market, knows where they all come from. If there's a town out on New Milo, they'd probably send folks out at least once in a while to trade for goods in Cinder Hill.

"I'll ask him about it next time we see him," Stoff says, and I catch just the barest edge of fatigue in his voice. It's understandable. I'm feeling it too, now, remembering why Bill is gone, why were up here talking about leaving instead of doing it. "You think he'll let us go tonight?"

"Hard to say." I leave it at that. It's the best I can offer. There's no reason to believe he won't. The drive out to Oborn Ferry is short by truck, maybe twenty or thirty minutes one way. If he's not back by lunch, I'll be surprised.

Stoff doesn't say anything else for a while after that. The silence between us is warm, comforting, but anxious traces still linger in the air. When the breezes coming in from the outside start to bring the sun's heat with them, I switch on the fan in the window again, park a chair next to it, watch people come and go in the street.

The kitchen peon doesn't come back to pick up our breakfast plate, leaves us hanging, wondering. For hours, there isn't much to do but wait, watch the town through the window as the sun makes a lazy trail to the high point of the sky, drops toward the west again.

Stoff naps, uses the time to catch up on his sleep. When lunch comes, it's late, maybe two or three in the afternoon. Pieces of local trout fried in oil pressed from blue flax, breaded with acorn frybread crumbs, a thin sauce that tastes kind of like basalmic vinegar but isn't. I catch the door before the kitchen rat can leave, smile at him, ask the guys outside if they've heard anything. They haven't. They're as in the dark as we are.

Hours pass. Stoff gets restless. I can't blame him. The night traffic on the street picks up again. It isn't as busy as it was Sunday night, but there are still enough people in town for the guy who runs The Mall to start up the generator, get the lights and music going. The playlist is a mix of southern rock, swamp rock, classic stuff from the sixties and seventies. It's nice, takes the edge off. When dinner comes, I talk to the guys at the door again. Still nothing, but they let me bum half a joint off them. Stoff and I pass it back and forth until it's gone, talk about getting more tomorrow. Weed's easy enough to come by in The Rift. It grows natural out here, pops up pretty much everywhere in Gold Country.

Dinner goes down easy – more breaded trout with more of that basalmic-like sauce. The heat of the day is still boiling off, and as it gets darker and the stars come out, Stoff and I start to talk again, talk about beer, about our last trip out to Napa Bay, the vintages we dredged out of a pressurized wine library that had managed to stay sealed until the day we cracked it. Neither of us brings up Bill. We're both thinking about him, about why no one seems to know anything, but neither of us puts the thoughts into words. *No point,* I tell myself. *Probably just sweating us. We'll see him in the morning.*

Across the street, the lights go out late. The Cinder Hill Inn has a power conservation policy that cuts the lights and fans off an hour or so after midnight on weekdays, but most folks aren't up that late. We are, and when it happens, there's really nothing else to do but crawl into bed with Stoff. We don't fuck, but we do get close. At some point in the night, he burrows his face into my shirt, shakes a little, but I can't tell if he's upset or if it's just a bad dream. Makes me a little uncomfortable, but I hold him, fall asleep again when the shaking stops and the muscles in his back go lax.

Chapter 12

I wake up a few hours after dawn, wake up sweating and hungry. Eyes bleary, I stumble out of bed, find the water carafe empty, look out the window. No way to tell what time it is, but the sun is up high enough that it's probably close to ten. A few hara hurry along the sidewalks, eager to get out of the building summer heat. One guy is pushing a wheelbarrow full of tin cans down the street. I watch him as he stops at the side door of the Inn, gives three knocks, waits until one of the kitchen guys comes along to help him unload.

Midweek in Cinder Hill. Another hour and the streets will be dead, empty. A few hara will weather the heat by crouching inside the dark, hollowed-out store fronts that cluster around the Inn and The Mall, but most of the county locals will be further up in the hills, cutting firewood where it's colder, tending fruit trees along the little meltwater creeks near settlements or watching crops in the lowlands and marshes near Jimtown. After the Sunday market, there's not much to do in the town itself but wait for dusk, for those brief few hours when the Thuulhuum come together to barter the day's goods for cold drinks and cheap entertainment.

Stoff wakes up maybe an hour after I do, lies there watching me while I stare out the window at the hills, at the buildings that were once tourist-trap stores full of knickknacks and bric-a-brac. Most of them are homes now, the plate glass windows broken and boarded, or bricked up to hide whole nests of hara that live together in spaces no bigger than five-hundred square feet in size.

The historic wood-plank sidewalks that used to meander from one end of main street to the other are all gone now, ripped up, long since burned as firewood, replaced with dirt or poorly-mixed concrete. Looking at it all, noting the changes, all the things that are different from the days when I was a kid, when I used to walk these same streets, used to buy licorice and comic books from the old man at Wolfe Drug Store a little further up the road – it gives me something to do. Not as entertaining as TV, but cable is only a memory now, and movies on disc or tape are hoarded like food.

"No word yet, huh?" Stoff asks, bringing me back. I shift in the creaking chair, lean back to look at him as he stretches, picks the sleep out of his eyes.

"No breakfast yet either," I gesture at the carafe, the empty table. Normally the kid from the kitchen comes early, just after the morning rush, but today – well, something else must be going on. Something outside the weekend usual. It's been a long time since I've been in Cinder Hill on a Tuesday, first time I've ever been locked up in a hotel room like this, waiting on room service.

"Think they forgot about us?" He tries something close to a grin, but it doesn't stick.

"Yeah." It comes on the edge of a laugh. "Sure."

"Maybe we can get another doob from the guys out there," he gestures.

"I'm already hungry, Stoff," I smile. "Last thing I need is–"

There's a knock. We both look up, go silent. For a moment, nothing happens. There's conversation, muffled, too quiet to hear, and then the door opens. One of the guys outside looks in, eyes flicking from mine to Stoff's.

"Bill wants to see you." His eyes flick back to mine.

"Downstairs."

"Fuckin– at last!" Stoff throws off the sheets, rolls off the bed, hands sweeping loose clothes up off the floor. I look at the guy in the doorway, nod.

"Give us a sec."

He nods back in response, simple, direct. I stand, pull on my shirt, look over at Stoff. Not much to gather up – just what we're wearing. Stoff buttons his jeans, looks over at me, meets my eyes as he pulls his own shirt on over his head.

"Tyse."

"Yeah?"

"I don't want to stop. . . what we've got," he manages. It comes out stiff, like he's hiding behind the words.

A little half smile peeks across my lips. I know how he feels, why it's so hard to say it.

"Okay," I nod. That easy, that simple.

Ragged tennis shoes, worn, dingy and soft from miles and miles on the road, slide easy over bare feet. A handful of seconds later and we're out the door, crossing the hallway with the guard-guy who gave me the joint. Two flights of stairs – red carpet, dull and tarnished brass banister, and then we're in the sawdust on the ground floor again. It's new, still smells fresh. Monday afternoons is usually when Bill has the week's batch burned and replaced, if I remember correctly.

Bill – we see him even before the guy escorting us gestures, falls away to the bar. The table where Bill is sitting is covered in yellowed scraps of paper weighed down by pocket-knife sharpened pencils. An old smartphone glows near his left hand, flashing figures. He looks up as we approach, puts the phone in standby to save power.

"Tyse, Stoff," he gestures. "Sit."

We do as we're told. Bill leans back in his chair, raises a hand, bends two fingers in a beckoning gesture. The bartender catches his meaning, nods, disappears into the kitchen.

"You hungry?" Bill asks us.

Stoff nods quickly. I lean back, give a casual bob of the chin. *Play it cool,* I tell myself, let my eyes narrow a little. *Play it like you're tired of his shit.*

"Food been alright the last couple of days?" He asks, leaning forward, peering at us over the rims of his glasses.

"Oh, it's – you've got a hell of a cook here, Bill," Stoff says.

Bill's eyes linger on me, on my eyes. I cross my arms for effect. "How about you, Tyse?" He asks. "Pleasant stay so far?"

"Pleasant?" I give him the edge of a laugh. "Yeah. Real pleasant being locked up in a room for a day and a half."

"Better than working for a living," he shoots back.

I ignore the remark. "What'd you find out Oborn Ferry?"

"Nothing." He turns back to his papers, lifts one, seems to study it. "Whole lot of nothing."

Nothing. I hesitate, lick my lips in the pause. Stoff looks at me, but I don't look back. I wait, try to pull some meaning out of the word. *Nothing.* Bill looks up, meets my eyes again.

"What do you mean," I try. "Nothing?"

"Nothing," he repeats. "I took two boys out on bikes. We went all the way out Oborn Ferry to Copperburg, caught the Four over that big hill out there, came back, didn't find a trace of anything on the road."

For a minute, we're dumbstruck. Stoff is the first one to speak, the first one to find his tongue.

"But–" he tries. "Bill, that's impossible. Tyse and I were both out there. The trucks – they were all over the road. There were chunks of metal and broken glass for a good five or six hundred feet in every direction."

"I believe it." Bill nods, looks back to the paper again. Stoff and I sit silent, waiting for Bill to continue. "Wouldn't have if the boys and I hadn't stopped off in Blackjack to poke around a few of the houses out there."

"Blackjack?" I look at Stoff, catch a glance, look back to Bill again. "You found the house we stayed in?"

"Nope. Wasn't looking for it." He exhales heavy, tired, looks up to meet my eyes again. "Blackjack's gone, Tyse. There's *nothing* there but a canyon road and some broken boards."

"Gone?" It takes a moment for the words to sink in. All those houses – they couldn't all have fallen into the reservoir in such a short period, could they?

"And it's not just Blackjack," Bill continues. "Copperburg, Quartz, all the little towns that used to be out there on that stretch of Oborn Ferry. All the little vacation spots, subdivisions, dead cars and abandoned trailer homes – all the metal, all the bolts, all the glass, all the plastic. It's all gone, like somebody stripped everything in a ten mile radius of that junction where the Four hits Oborn Ferry."

It's unreal. There are no words. Bill looks at me for a long time, and for a moment I think I see the traces of fear behind the facade, behind the expression of fatherly concern he wears like a mask.

"I've never seen anything like it in my life," he adds.

"Gotta be aliens," Stoff says. Both Bill and I look at

him. "Well," he shrugs. "What else?"

"Some new gang," Bill offers. "Some very detail-oriented folks who do quick work, have some use for all that metal and plastic and glass they took."

"I dunno, Bill," I find myself saying, almost regret it when he turns his eyes on me again. I open my hands in a receptive gesture, smile, leave it at that.

"It's weird, I'll admit it," Bill says, eyes going back to Stoff, "but I ain't ever met anyone who's claimed to have seen aliens who wasn't absolutely as crazy as catshit." He shifts a little, leans back in his chair again. "Look, I'd be lying if I said that the whole thing doesn't make me nervous as hell. I damn near blew half my stockpile of cans and madrone cider this morning just getting a bunch of armed guys together to watch the roads for the next few weeks. Something serious is going on out there, and I want Cinder Hill to be as ready as we can be when the chips hit the fan."

Armed guys. After seeing what happened to Davy, I don't envy anyone Bill's got watching the roads. Just thinking about it makes me want to get as far away from Oborn Ferry as I can, take Stoff with me, maybe push east and hide out way up in the mountains, watch whatever's meant to happen from a distance. Stoff seems to pick up on my thoughts, glances over at me, gets cut off before he can speak.

"I've still got some routes that need watching," Bill offers, smiling a little. At that moment, the bartender arrives with a tray full of plates and porcelain dishware. The timing is perfect, the meal more lavish than anything I've seen this close since I was human. Breakfast – a full breakfast, not just leftovers, and a plate for each of us. Warm sugar-pine syrup dripping across a short stack of acorn pancakes slathered with goat butter. A trio of pork sausages next to a pile of blackberries and sliced Indian Free Peaches. The icing on the cake is a big thermos of something dark like coffee, but richer. When the bartender pours it into mugs, I catch notes of fennel, cinnamon, but other than that, I honestly couldn't tell you what all's in it. All I know is it's good, damn good. No one eats like this without a great trade on the line. Bill needs more guys, and I'm guessing that with a meal like this, I won't be getting my gun back.

Doesn't bother me. It's almost worth it. Gun never really was mine to begin with anyway.

"Pay isn't much," Bill continues as he digs in, slides a butter knife through his own stack of pancakes, cuts wedges, spears them with his fork. "two meals, half-gallon of water and a drink for each of you." He takes a bite, chews it, swallows, adds, "that's the daily wage."

"Actually, uh, Bill," Stoff speaks up again. I look over, realize he hasn't touched his food yet. He's waiting for the other shoe to drop. He's afraid of the hook that might come with the meal. I don't care. Never been anyone who could make me do something I don't want to do. I start with the most expensive part of the meal – the sausages. "See, Tyse and I have been talking. We're thinking about packing up and heading out to a smaller settlement." He pauses a moment, almost as if testing the waters. Bill just looks at him, chewing, waiting. "Uh, didn't you say once that there was a little group of guys that strung together a bunch of old houseboats on New Milo?"

"I didn't, but I've heard some folks went out that way." Bill says, tone flat. "They're way out on the lake from what I've been told. Need a boat to get out there."

"Right." Stoff forces a smile. I watch him, move on to

my own stack of pancakes. "You wouldn't, uh, know anybody out there, would you?"

"Personally, no," Bill looks down at his food, sighs, considering, looks back up again. "I know that a pair of guys comes in almost every week for the Sunday market. They bring fish from the lake. If you stick around until Sunday, I'll feed you both and you can talk to them when they show up."

"Stick around for road-duty," I put in. Both guys look at me. It takes a moment, but Bill finally nods. I smile around a mouthful of the food. "It's a kind offer, Bill, but Stoff and I have seen these guys up close already and have no desire to do so again anytime soon." The idea of regular meals is tempting, but not tempting enough. I look at Stoff. "It's a hike, but I'm sure they need help out at the Segerstrom ranch this time of year." I look at Bill again. "We could put in the rest of the week there. Regular meals, good company, a bus that comes into town for the Sunday market and no chance of death at the hands of some crazy gang."

Stoff watches me, swallows. Bill looks at me for a long time, finally shrugs, turns back to his meal.

"Suit yourselves," is all he says. No hook then, no negotiation, and I'm definitely not getting my gun back. I fork another chunk of pancake into my mouth, gesture to Stoff. He picks up his own silverware almost reluctantly, looks at Bill, but Bill doesn't look back. No shortage of hungry hara looking for an easy meal, then. Bill probably thought he was doing us a favor, getting a couple of guys slightly smarter than the average running dummy in trade for a breakfast with a few ingredients that probably would have gone bad before the weekend anyway.

"Eat up," Bill says to Stoff, forces a smile. "Segerstrom

Ranch is about a twenty mile walk from here, and there's not a lot to eat in between."

"Feels like it's going to be a scorcher today too," I smile, pour myself a cup of the coffee-stuff, salute Bill before I drink. "Here's to you. Hell of a breakfast!"

"We aim to please," he grumbles.

CHAPTER 13

Even after resting for two days and change, my feet are still sore. I don't really start to feel it until we're about four miles up from the center of Cinder Hill, and ten miles in we're both limping again. Bill's right– not a lot to eat on the road. Hara living in the old shops that rise up along the curb as we make our way east have picked all the blackberry bushes clean, chewed the chamomile, the fennel and everything else down to the nub. A skinny goat bleats at us from a pen as we pass, nuzzles the wire. Mid-summer, and things are getting a little lean along the well-traveled paths. Still plenty to eat, but you've got to walk further and further out to get at it.

The road is hot, but the flat, direct course it cuts through the foothills makes it preferable to cresting every rise between Cinder Hill and the Segerstrom Ranch. The curbs are all gravel, some short, others big as parking lots, but all of them are edged either by a slope, a cliff or a building. Not a lot of trees along the road either. Fair amount of stumps, but stumps don't make any shade. With no water to sip during the walk, all we can do is sweat and suffer – and eventually, the sweat runs out.

The sun is sliding west, halfway to the horizon when we reach the last rise of road before Segerstrom Ranch. The old sign that used to advertise train rides and orchard tours has long since been torn down, but I recognize the curve, the long stretch of road before the lane that cuts off into a smattering of live oak, darts north toward the ranch. Lot of fond memories of visiting Segerstrom as a kid, back when it was just an apple farm run by some godly group about one step away from the Amish in their level of devotion. I share some of the memories with Stoff, get nods and grins that help both of us make the last half mile or so we have to walk.

At its peak, Segerstrom Ranch spanned a huge area–couldn't say how big, but the family that owned it had kept it running since the gold rush days. Most of the Segerstroms either disappeared, moved on or died when everything fell apart, but a few of the younger guys are still around. Under their leadership, it's expanded out into a number of the neighboring properties, now feeds and employs a good portion of the hara in the hollow hills. The dress code is looser, the folks that work there less rigid than those who once owned it. It's more like a hippy commune now, actually. Before, you'd never see any of the Segerstrom boys running around with anything less than beards and thick flannel shirts. These days, those who live and work with the Segerstroms all run around in tie-dye and hemp, if they wear anything at all.

Following the road makes us nice and obvious. A pair of hara meet us a couple hundred feet from the barricade that blocks the road on the south-side entrance to the ranch. Wary smiles, extended hands, hip-holstered six-shooters nice and obvious. They don't get many gangs or ferals this far east. Too cold, but that doesn't mean it never happens. I take it as a courtesy, let them check us out, answer their questions honestly, evenly, make it clear we're just passing through.

It's enough. They're a kind-hearted bunch, welcome us with open arms. One of the guys inside the barricade recognizes me, shakes my hand, offers to introduce us to everyone. Jeff, that's his name. I grin at his long, brown-blond dreadlocks, the way he stops to kiss another dude so passionately it makes my toes curl a little. Different times, different values. Sometimes it's hard seeing how much the county has changed. Sometimes it's almost funny.

The day goes easy. Jeff leads us out to the fields, has us run baskets of white and yellow peaches back to the ranch's "kitchen-house" for processing. The smell is incredible – three big pots of jam boil on range stoves powered by a wood-burning kit generator. A pair of tall, friendly guys stripped to the skivvies and sweating with the heat take the baskets from us, grin at us, check us out in ways that are pretty obvious, if not a little uncomfortable.

A few hours – that's about how long the work lasts before dusk comes and the picking wraps up for the day. For dinner, the whole ranch gathers at a series of rough picnic tables outside, shares heaping plates of salted pork and a salad made from bear weed, buckbrush and miner's lettuce. Peach cobbler and peach pie are brought out for dessert, but it's the wine that Stoff and I can't get enough of. It's sweet, almost syrupy, a dark red in color and very strong. Jeff tells us it's a concoction invented by one of the Segerstrom boys, something made from dogwood berries and sugar-pine sap.

By the time the stars come out, everyone's either drunk, high or both. The atmosphere is loose, the generators are silent, and the sound of drums and acoustic guitars echoes through the hills. People are dancing, rise and writhe as elegant black shapes backlit by roaring firelight. Somehow I end up kissing Stoff, pressing him into the grass on a cool hillside surrounded by fragrant trees heavy with peaches. The sounds of celebration rise and roar as we make love, release our need together, stare up at the stars with sweaty, heaving chests.

Every day on the Segerstrom ranch goes like that. The first night, we sleep on the ground, but freezing your ass off on the dirt all night and waking up sweaty isn't as romantic as it seems like it might be when you haven't done it in a while. Wednesday night, we make a point of dragging ourselves to an empty cot in the bunkhouse near the far north end of the ranch, claim it for the rest of the week. I recognize the building when we wake up in it on Thursday morning. Keenan's Rehab, or at least it used to be. Lot of beds, lot of space. Lot of art on the concrete walls that wasn't there before the Segerstrom Ranch claimed it.

Stoff and I spend Wednesday running peaches to the kitchen-house again. Instead of being made into jam, most of these are pureed and set up to sun-dry into fruit leather. Thursday we head out with a group of guys leading a team of horses and pack mules, help them gather firewood a little further up the road, a mile or two north-east of the ranch. Friday morning it's egg-duty, guard duty and compost-turning. Around the ranch, chores change like that. Rarely is anyone ever doing the same thing all the time.

When Saturday finally comes and the ranch is abuzz with excitement about the Sunday market, Stoff and I take a moment to consider our future. We both know we don't have to go back into Cinder Hill. Segerstrom Ranch always needs guys willing to stay behind, walk the perimeter while everyone else is at the market. Jeff wants us to stay. Hell, pretty much everybody on the ranch wants us to stick around, live there, even. We're useful, hard working and fun, or so they say. It's tempting. It's definitely tempting.

In the end, though, the idea of living on the water again wins out. Neither Stoff or I knows what to expect out there, but Jeff makes it clear that if things aren't as great as we're hoping for them to be, there will always be room for us out at Segerstrom. It's nice to know, helps a little.

Saturday's wash day for us. There's a creek about a half mile to the east, and the cold water feels good on our hands even if we do spend half the day scrubbing hemp rags against rocks. Lunch is roasted soaproot and blackberries, all picked near the stream, and while we eat, we spend about an hour just sitting in the stony shallows, smoking joints and trading stories from the time before things fell apart.

Making dinner falls to us as well, but with ten folks working on it, things come together easy. Another salad, another set of platters heaped with salted pork. I spend most of the time just looking for something to do, finally get sent off to a field to pick more miner's lettuce. The leaves I find are succulent, green and delicious. I eat a few while I'm picking them, savor the taste, knowing I might never get a chance to do so again.

Dinner is bittersweet. Jeff sits with us again, but none of us talks much. As night falls and we all get tipsy, he leads us to one of the fire pits, hands Stoff a goatskin drum, hands me this weird instrument that looks like a wooden toad with a stick in its guts. People start to hum, sing, chant, beat on their own drums, and Jeff shows me how to play the toad. Apparently the stick comes out, makes a neat noise when you run it across the toad's spiny back.

Eventually, Jeff rises, dances closer to the fire with the guy he's taken as his girl. The guy he's chosen to *be* with. Whatever you want to call it. They kiss, dance apart, dance with their palms touching, grinning the whole time. Part of me is uncomfortable with the whole thing, but more and more I find myself happy for both of them, for myself, for Stoff and all the others. We were all men. We were all, or almost all, straight men before we were incepted. It's weird, but comforting, witnessing hara being hara. It's like the parties I used to go to when I was younger, parties full of drunk guys and easy girls – except the lines are blurred now. We're all drunk guys as much as we are easy girls. We fill both roles. We're as free and feminine as we are rigid and male.

Stoff comes to me then, silences my thoughts with a deep kiss. The heat of his lips, the passion – I get swept up in it, lost in it. Time becomes a blur, the night and fire a roar. We make love right there in the drum circle and no one takes offense. It's normal, animal, *freeing*. When it's over and we're leaning into each other, trying to catch our breath, I see Jeff grin at us, just for an instant, then disappear behind the flames with his lover, the two sprinting off into the night together.

I don't sleep much that night. I think long and hard about staying, about talking Stoff into staying. Wouldn't take much prodding to get him on board, but the allure of living on the water eventually pulls me back. In the darkness, I listen to the sounds of crickets and bats, pick out the distant hoots of owls. At some point, there's whispering, the creaking of springs, little moans, but it doesn't last long. A pair of mountain lions calling to each other comes shortly after, fades as they get closer to each other, further away from the ranch.

Morning comes too bright, too early. Stoff wakes me up with a cup of Mormon tea sweetened with a dollop of strawberry jam, leads me to the picnic tables for breakfast. Market day's first meal is light–poached eggs seasoned with spicy ground bladderpod seed, slices of white and yellow peaches on the side. Last chore before we leave is dishes – quick, easy. Many hands make light work.

Jeff doesn't ride into town with us. He stays at the ranch with a cadre of guys who've volunteered to hold down the fort while the rest of us hit the Sunday market. Doesn't take long to load the old bio-diesel powered school bus with the trade goods for the day, and the smell of all that food is intoxicating. We work down the windows when we finally hit the road, savor the cool breezes of another hot, summer morning.

Twenty miles, give or take a few thousand feet. It's a lot easier, goes a lot quicker when you do it by bus instead of on foot. Stoff and I sit quiet, watch the live oak as it thins more and more the closer we get to Cinder Hill. There's actually traffic when we get to the last few miles – horses, mules, hatchbacks and beat-up pickups. Everybody's creeping along, waiting. A couple of enterprising guys wade through it all with bare feet, offer sweets and cold booze for steep trades.

I look out the window at the sky, see nothing but blue, the white-gray traces of a cloud, so thin it's barely visible. No birds. The sun's still low on the horizon.

"Seems like there's some kind of problem up ahead," the guy driving the bus says. I look over at him, at his tanned legs, the grungy foam flip-flops that were once some neon shade of green. A short brown ponytail hangs out of the back of his red, mesh trucker cap. The tattoo on his arm says *Lev. 19:28.*

Smoke drifts across the sky beyond the windshield. I sit up a little, look over the tangle of hara migrating toward the last long, blind curve before the descent into Cinder Hill from the eastern road. Nobody's moving. All any of us can see is the pavement, the hills on either side of it, the smoke.

And that's when it happens.

"What – the – fuck. . .?" the driver stretches out the syllables, shifts the sugar-pine gumwad he's been chewing on around in his mouth. A few of the guys in seats look at each other, a few stand. The smoke surges, and then the road coming out of the blind curve is a swarming, seething mass of movement. The driver's hand goes for the gearshift, sits on it, fingers curved and ready, apprehensive. Stoff sits up next to me, looks at me as I stand, step into the central walkway.

The whole thing devolves into a shit-storm before anyone can react, do anything about it. Motionless vehicles, patient horses and mules – in an instant, they're all moving, pushing, darting wildly, careening into each other. The chaos turns into a tangled mess of squealing metal and screaming – and then I see it, high in the sky, diving like a hawk.

An airplane. Something like an airplane, black and glossy, fire leaping from its wings.

"We gotta go," I tell the bus driver, turn to look at him. "We gotta go – now!"

He nods in response, once, quickly. "I hear that!" One smooth movement kicks the bus into reverse, sets the wheels moving. I hear cars honking, hara yelling, but I don't care. Stoff shouts something as I run to the open door of the bus, jump out on the pavement, start waving my arms in an attempt to clear the traffic behind us.

When the first explosion goes off, the sound is incredible. Wind whips my hair and I turn, see a ball of black smoke and fire rising toward the sky. The plane makes no noise as it darts overhead, but the screaming that follows in its wake is deafening. Too shocked to yell, I watch the plane rise again, corner machine-precise to the south.

Stoff shouts my name and it brings me back. The bus is moving, and the folks behind us are doing everything they can to get out of our way, but it's not enough. Panic has set in. People are gunning throttles, scaring their horses into snarls of meat and metal thick enough to keep us trapped. I look back toward the curve just in time to see the first wave of hara swarming toward us, trying to get away from whatever's going down in Cinder Hill. Someone sprints past me, bumps me hard enough to knock me into the bus. Stoff shouts again, but I stand in the rushing wave of bodies, one hand on the bus, realize immediately how hosed we are.

"We've got to leave the bus," I breathe, more to myself than to anyone else. The realization brings me back, brings my eyes to Stoff's. "We've got to leave the bus!" I shout. "Stoff! Get everyone off the bus!"

I expect some kind of protest, a grumble, something, but it's quickly clear to everyone that the bus isn't going anywhere all knotted up in the chaos like it is. A few seconds, and everyone's on the ground, on the hot tarmac, looking around, uncertain. Panicked people push us apart, pass through like bullets as they sprint away from Cinder Hill. I look back, feel momentarily lost.

And then that first round catches some terrified kid right in the back of the skull as he's running toward us, drops him instantly. The shot is even, precise. The exit wound turns his face into a ragged mess, and instantly I'm thinking of Davy, of *that day*. The glitter and shine of steel and black glass flashes amongst the vehicles, sends a fresh stab of panic thrilling through me. They move fast – *Jesus, they move fast*. I look to the eastern road, to the open hills beyond the bus, hope the gang that's tearing through the cars and hara closer to Cinder Hill hasn't been smart enough to send a flanking force to catch us when we run.

"Move!" I shout suddenly. It works, startles everyone out of their daze. When they move, they follow me, become one with the sprinting wave that washes over and between the stalled wrecks of cars, the twitching bodies of pack animals, their crushed riders. We don't stop to help anyone. The gunfire behind us keeps us moving, and the one time I glance back to look at the mess on the road, I can see a swarm of them, can see *so many* of those masked bastards tearing through the traffic, shoving aside cars, slaughtering those stupid enough to stay and fight, those unlucky enough to get left behind.

"Run!" I yell, and we do. We run as hard as we can, and still–

Still, it's not enough.

Chapter 14

In the beginning, there's this vague idea in my head that we might follow the road back to Segerstrom Ranch, hole up there and wait for the fuckers to come and face us on our turf. It's a misguided idea, not even fully thought out, with no real plan or logical sense to support it. It's the only thing that comes to me when we're running, the only place that seems like it might be safe.

In reality, most of us don't even make it out of Cinder Hill. The guns are fast, terrifyingly precise. I see the guy off to my left go down with a single shot, just fall away into nothingness. I don't stop, but I catch sight of the guy who does. He doesn't even have time to crouch or call out. A bullet drops him, splits his skull without warning, leaves him gurgling, convulsing on the pavement.

Stoff is beside me. Another guy falls, just drops, faceplants against the side of a truck, doesn't get up. All I can think about is getting Stoff to safety. All I can think about is surviving. Another shot, and then there are only five of us.

We hit a line of cars, vault over, all of us except the bus driver. I see it out of the corner of my eye, watch him spin and fall sideways when he catches a bullet. Somewhere behind us, there's another blast – loud, the wind whipping up, hot and thick with the smell of sulfur. I run harder, run as fast as I can. Stoff starts to slow, but I grab him by the collar and force him to run faster.

One more knot of cars and we're on open tarmac again. Dumbstruck hara stand on the pavement, sit atop horses, stare from the windows of jam-packed sedans.

Someone shouts at us, but it doesn't come through the panic as anything more than noise.

The quick *zwip* of a bullet cutting through the engine block of a truck is all it takes. The truck stalls out, the guy inside starts yelling, and then everyone turns just in time to see the second round plaster his brains across the glass.

Like quail, everyone takes flight. Horses and cars scatter into the nearest intersection, dart up either side of the side-road. Some rush east at full speed. I see a round shred a tire, spin a truck into a pair of mules. Neither the driver or the guy walking the mules lives long enough to yell about it.

Cover becomes a priority. As the thinner traffic turns and floors it for the hills, the guns shift their focus to the big trucks, the cars – anything metal, and the more the better. More hara fall, but by some miracle, Stoff and I manage to stay one step ahead of the rounds, manage to catch enough cover to keep from catching a bullet to the brainpan. Somewhere along the way, I realize that we've lost all of the guys from Segerstrom Ranch. *All of them.* We're alone, and the rounds keep coming.

When we hit the first downhill slope off the right side of the road, we run for it. The sound of rounds cutting air is close, but they're still tracking other targets, silencing the cars, the trucks, the mules with saddlepacks full of copper wire and other scrap. I hear the quick hornet whine of a dirtbike as it spins out, glance back just in time to see the back tire flying apart, throwing rubber. The rider only has about enough time to brace himself on the bars before his helmet bounces with the impact of a round, spurts crimson.

We don't stick around, don't see him fall. The hill is more of a scarp – the gravel drive beside a furniture outlet. The bulk of the building blocks out some of the noise, makes for great cover, but the footing is loose, almost drops us as we stumble down to a gravel lot that wraps around behind the outlet, come up against a barbed wire fence, pitch ourselves over into a ditch.

We're down for a breath or less – I reach out, drag Stoff to his feet, practically haul him as he struggles to keep up with me. Fifteen feet of darker slate gravel and we're on the rail-tracks that cross through Cinder Hill, looking west, looking east.

For a brief moment, I almost feel safe. I recognize this stretch of tracks, know how far in either direction it goes. There's smoke in the sky, plumes coming up from the center of town, but with trees, hills and a line of storefronts blocking the chaos on the road, it all seems so far away now. The sounds of gunfire come only as occasional cracks, the rattle of weapons barking quick, going silent.

"What are you doing?" Stoff asks. I look at him, catch the terror on his face, come back suddenly. Eyes hit the tracks. The rails – they wander, cut a curving course between hillsides, but the route will carry us vaguely east, drop us off about eight miles from Segerstrom Ranch when we reach the last curve where the tracks cut north, dead-end at the mill. Long way to run, but–

"Tyse!" He shouts, starts trotting east, looks back at me but doesn't wait. I take the cue, push myself to catch up with him.

I'm not looking ahead. I'm glancing to the right, to the rows of roofs, the old shops and stores rising up from flats long ago terraced into a hillside that descends from the rail bed, sweeps down toward the Eighty-Eight. No one on the highway, no sign of anyone or anything on the long, straight lanes in between. All the activity is behind us, spreading out from the Sunday market. Hope sticks with me as we move. The rail is low enough, the rise between us and the carnage is steep enough that we might just make it. We might just slip out, slip away, get back to Segerstrom Ranch in time to warn them.

Stoff stops. He's still a pace or two ahead of me, but as I reach out, put a hand on his trembling back, he starts again, takes a step forward. I open my mouth to ask what's wrong, never get the chance.

A hand is the first thing I see. A hand, fingers curled, wet with the running lines of drying blood. A face, eyes vacant and staring. *Five faces* – all cracked like ripe melons, open to the sun.

I put a hand over my mouth, try not to vomit. Stoff stumbles off the tracks, blows chunks into the weeds. There are five of them sprawled upright, three more flipped over– all dead, all sprawled across the rails, all cut down with clean shots that cut right between the eyes. The wounds are fresh, precise. I look up in terror, and then one of *them* comes stumbling out of a stand of trees, one leg crunchy, wobbling, glass mask cracked and leaking darkness.

There's no time, no time to shout. I do the only thing that seems right. I leap at him, throw myself at the dark knot that looks like a weapon bound up in his bent fingers. He reacts immediately. I never even see the blow coming.

The crunchy leg is probably the only thing that saves me. The punch hits me square in the upper arm instead of in the face, knocks me backward. The pain is incredible, almost blinds me – and then I trip over the closest rail, fall sprawling across gravel.

There's a terrible moment when all I can see is that gun, that cracked mask, that wobbling leg. I know I'm going to die. I know it's close. The shot takes a moment to line up, but he's careful, quick. The leg only slows him down a little. The barrel of the gun is cold chrome.

That's when Stoff comes out of nowhere. For an instant, he's like a blur of light and movement, and then the guy with the cracked mask turns at the hip, swings the gun up, fires. The shot is hasty, it goes wide, doesn't even clip Stoff. Flat hands come up against black glass, fingers curling into the cracks. The guy with the mask doesn't get a chance to throw him off.

There's a flash, bright and violent. I see Stoff's teeth, bared and snarling, his wild hair wind-whipped. Heat blossoms out from the point where hands touch glass, and then the guy with the mask is reeling, spitting sparks. Electric fire gouts from the cracks in the mask, and then Stoff screams, shoves hard. The clank and sputter of the body hitting the dirt is loud, sounds like a crate of salvage hitting pavement.

For a moment, nothing happens. It's a long moment, painful, stretching. Stoff looks at me, and I can see the black marks seared into his palms. He comes back to reality first, rips up his shirt, binds his hands with it, then offers me one. "Come on," he says. "We should go before any more show up."

I don't speak. I can't. There's nothing to say. The whole time we're running, following the tracks east, all I can think about is the flash of light, the moment when Stoff's hands caught that glass mask and filled it with fire. It doesn't make sense, seems like something you might see in a movie, not something you'd ever see in real life. My whole arm hurts like hell, hurts too much to move, and the pain distracts me, keeps me quiet. Stoff doesn't say anything either. He runs like it never happened, or maybe, like it *did*, like he's running from it.

The rails weave left, weave right. The sounds of conflict fall off, die away. Neither of us looks back. We just run. We run until the rail wraps itself around the shopping center on the eastern outskirts of Cinder Hill, and we keep running. Occasionally, we see a knot of hara, of guys on horses or in cars, trucks, on bikes idling catty-corner in the road, but it's clear that no one is headed toward the center of town anymore, to the market. Enough people have gotten away to warn the rest, to warn the latecomers. I try not to think about how many people are dead, how many were caught and massacred today before we even arrived, how many more were killed when we ran.

The rail runs east, comes within a quarter mile of the road again before it sweeps north toward the mill. Stoff and I run out of steam long before then, limp the rest of the way to the curve, then cross a field of dry, waist-high grass just as the day really starts to get hot. We're both thirsty, shaky with adrenaline, sore in the feet, but still we keep moving. My arm is numb now, still aches, throbs, but most of the time I don't feel it. *Doesn't matter*, I keep telling myself. *Gotta keep moving. Gotta get to the ranch. Gotta warn the others.*

Eight miles. Eight miles of hot, twisting, ever-rising road carries us into the higher hills, into places where we can get a little shade from the scraggly live oaks that come up close to the curb. It's the hottest part of the day by the time we reach the barricades at the south end of Segerstrom Ranch, stumble, almost collapse in the road as a pair of guys jogs out to meet us. Their eyes are wary, worried. Someone calls for Jeff, brings us water. "What happened?" someone else asks. I shake my head, wince when a hand touches my hanging arm. Stoff takes a bottle of water in shaking hands, practically dumps it all over his face. I'm more careful, suck greedily at the weathered plastic while he exhales wetly, wipes at his nose.

"They're here," Stoff says, and everyone looks up, looks at him. "The gang that hit us on the road, the guys that killed Hima. They took Cinder Hill. They killed everyone. *They're here!*"

CHAPTER 15

We don't talk about what happened on the tracks. We don't talk about the flash of light, the way Stoff blasted that guy, set him *on fire* with a *touch*, but it's on my mind the whole time. When Stoff speaks, he tells them about the chaos on the road into town, the shots, watching guys take bullets, fall, how powerless we were to help them, to do anything but *run*. Jeff makes silent gestures while the words fall from Stoff's mouth, leads us across the ranch to the bunkhouse. Cots are cleared for both of us, side-by-side, and Stoff keeps talking even after we've sat. Hara run back and forth while Jeff listens. Some of the guys are carrying rifles, others gather in knots, trading quick, quiet words before breaking apart again, rushing off somewhere else.

Eventually, someone comes to look at my arm. "Dislocated," he whispers, then stands, takes a firm grip on it. "This is gonna hurt," he says, and I nod, close my eyes. The pain comes quick, sudden, and I grit my teeth against it, but it passes again just as quickly, leaves a cool wash of relief in its wake. I thank the guy, but he only pats my other shoulder, moves on. Jeff looks me over briefly, eyes concerned, then turns back to Stoff.

"They're going to come here too," I say suddenly. Jeff looks back at me again, but I don't meet his eyes, just keep mine focused on the concrete floor of the bunkhouse. The air is hot, but the shade is nice, takes some of the edge off. Stoff's steady, frightened monologue winds down, starts to spin apart – and when I look up, they're both staring at me, watching me. A couple of other guys are standing a handful of feet away from us, listening in while pretending to be busy. "They hit Cinder Hill, but they won't stop there. There's no reason for them to stop there."

"We're a long way out," Jeff says, tries to make it sound dismissive.

"Half a day," I shake my head. "Not all that far."

"Then we'll be ready," Jeff tries. I catch the tremble in his voice, and it forces the edges of a smile across my lips.

"Cinder Hill was ready." I don't look at him, can't look at him. "Bill had people watching all of the roads, people with guns. There were so many of them, *so many*, but now they're all – they're all –"

"Then what do you suggest we do?" Jeff shoots back, angry now. Can't blame him. I don't know. I shake my head, start to laugh, but it just makes him madder. "Tyse! Dammit, Tyse!"

"We can't stay here," Stoff says suddenly. He's shaking now, shivering despite the heat.

Jeff turns on him, bares teeth, barks words. "Yeah? Where do we go, then?" He shakes his head, makes a frustrated gesture. "We just lost a dozen of our people. We lost our bus. We lost an entire week's worth of trade!" He looks back at me again, growls, "We can't lose this ranch. It's all we have left, Tyse. *It's all we have left.*"

"You don't understand." I look at Jeff again, meet his stare evenly. "I've seen what they can do. Last week, I watched one tear out Davy's face. This morning, I watched hara fall by the dozens. I saw guys drop from horses that were at full gallop, take rounds right to the center of the head from a hundred yards or more away. Most of the guys who died never even saw the gun that dropped them– the shots were that precise."

"And they have airplanes," Stoff puts in.

"Military airplanes." I nod. "They were dropping *bombs*, Jeff."

"Yeah." Jeff sighs loudly, looks away. "You keep talking about how badass these fuckers are. You keep telling me *we're next.*" He pauses, looks back. "Look, okay, we can't fight them, and it sounds like if we run, they'll just kill us somewhere else." He makes another frustrated gesture. "What *can* we do?"

There's a long moment of silence. Stoff suddenly breaks, starts to cry. I have nothing. Finally Jeff stands up, curses, bares teeth at the floor. When he turns back to the bunkhouse door, he catches sight of the two guys who've been listening to the whole thing, fixes them with a sharp stare.

"Get everyone together. We need ideas. We need to group-think this out, come up with a plan." The two guys look at each other, nod, but they're too slow for Jeff. "Get moving!" He yells, and it seems to do the trick. They're gone in another instant, and then we're alone with Jeff.

"You two need to pull yourselves together," he says to us, still standing, watching us without fully looking at us. I find myself staring at the gun holstered at his side, close my eyes, shake my head. Can't take the easy way out. Never could.

Jeff takes a step toward Stoff, drops to a crouch beside him, puts hands on his shoulders. "I know it was bad. I know you saw things – things no one should see. I know you think we're *fucked*, but we're not. As long as we're alive, there's hope, but *dammit.*" He looks at me then. "I need both of you. You're the only ones I know who've seen these things. What you know, however little you may think it is, might be the key to the only shot we have of killing them before they kill us."

"It won't matter," Stoff burbles. "It–"

"It *does* matter!" Jeff barks back, shakes Stoff. The violence of the action awakens something in me, and then I'm looking at the gun at his side again. *Don't do it.* I lick my lips. Jeff bares teeth at *my man*, my drinking buddy, the guy I love. "Stoff! Man up, dammit! We need you!"

I'm on my feet before I realize it. Jeff looks at me, and suddenly there's fear in his eyes. I don't move, don't say anything, but he gets it. He takes the hint, backs off a little. Stoff's the closest thing I have to a woman, and Jeff sees it, knows it, knows what he'd do if he were in my shoes, if his woman were crying, if I were yelling at her, shaking her, making it worse.

"Tyse," he says. Just that, just my name, like a whisper. I see the fear in his eyes. It's enough. I look away reflexively. All the fire is gone, the fear replaced by numbness, fatigue. Stoff rubs at his eyes with his fingers, almost as if he's trying to jam the tears back in.

"Okay," I breathe. When I look at him again, Jeff swallows, takes a breath. His eyes are wider now, more wary. It takes me a moment to find my voice, to find the words.

"Maybe there's a way," I try, don't believe the words even as I say them. "Maybe."

"That's better," Jeff says. It isn't condescending, the way he puts it out there. It's hopeful, encouraging. I think about the flash of light again, the fire shooting from the cracks in the glass faceplate of that guy, that *thing* that tried to kill us on the tracks and I almost open my mouth, but I can't figure out how to put it into words. Stoff sniffs, looks up, speaks before I figure it out.

"They aren't human. They aren't har, but they can be

killed, I think." He says. Jeff and I both look at him, watch him as he rubs at his eyes with shaky hands again. "Something happened when we were out there. Something I don't understand."

Jeff waits for more, eventually looks back at me with questioning eyes. I have no answer for him, only meet his stare. In the silence, footsteps signal the approach of other guys. Faces peek in at us. Before long, Jeff breaks the stare, catches the eyes of the newcomers, gestures them into the room.

"Think on it," he says to me, glances at Stoff. As guys gather around us, lean against the concrete walls, Jeff slips out, leaves us there in the uncomfortable silence that follows. Only when the bunkhouse is packed does he return again, and even then, he has eyes only for the other ranch hands, doesn't look at me or Stoff.

Faces peer in from doorways leading to other rooms. Some of the younger guys sit on the floor. One chews a wad of sugar-pine sap and it makes me think of the bus driver we lost. There are probably two dozen of us in all. Not many, but a crowd when we're all jammed into the closest thing the bunkhouse has to a parlor.

"Let's talk ideas," Jeff begins, and in the silence that follows, I look at Stoff, find his eyes, the pain there, the fear, the numbness. Nobody says anything for a long while. Nobody wants to be the first to speak. Can't blame them. Can't blame any of them.

Word's already gotten around, and nobody really thinks we have a prayer.

Not even Jeff, I reckon.

CHAPTER 16

When the conversation starts, it starts slow. Jeff practically has to drag a few guys out by name to get them to speak, get the ball rolling. The ideas are simple at first, almost painful to hear. "We got about, uh – seven twenty-two rifles," one guy ventures. "Few hundred rounds. Ten thirty-eight revolvers, say ten dozen rounds. One four-ten with about two rounds of bird shot left. One thirty-aught with about ten rounds. Lot of knives."

"We can rig up some spears using the knives," another guy tries, puts the idea out there only after being prodded. "Give us, uh, better reach?"

"We can't fight them like that," I finally bite back. *Too harsh.* All eyes are on me now. "The gang that took Cinder Hill – they're crack shots, every single one of them. They could kill every one of us before we'd even see them coming, and you want to use *spears?*"

The spear-guy seems at a loss for words for a moment. Eyes flick between him and me, curious, uncertain. "Well, uh, if we was to hide in a ditch, maybe," he sputters, trying again. "We could surprise them, pop out once they pass and then stab them all in the back!"

"There's got to be a better plan than that," Stoff puts in.

"Well, I don't see y'all coming up with one!" The guy shoots back, red in the face, waving his finger at us.

"Garse," one of the guys leaning against the wall unfolds his arms, gestures, catches the attention of a har across the room from him. "You know those two trucks down by the creek?" Garse sits up, nods. "What would it take to get those running again?"

E. S. Wynn

"Uh," Garse hesitates, thinks about it for a moment. "Well, one needs a new battery. Tires are probably shot. The other blew a head before we parked it. Tires are probably shot on that one too."

"We've got that bike," another guy puts in. "The one in the barn, one we used to use to run jars of jam and pick up seeds at the market with before we had the bus."

"Bikes and trucks are the first things they shoot at." I kill that idea, get pained looks in the pause.

"Sounds like the trucks need too much work anyway," Jeff says, nods at the guy who mentioned the bike. "The bike. It runs? You could take it out today?"

"Well, I'd have to look at it, but yeah. Probably, yeah."

"There's a Varr camp in Reagan Meadows, just over the pass." Jeff fixes the guy with a direct look. "If we can find enough fuel, would you be willing to take one other guy and let them know what's going on out here? See if we can't work out some kind of trade deal for assistance?"

"Sure." The guy nods, looks worried, hesitates, swallows. "Sure. Might could."

"Good," Jeff turns back to the others, meets my eyes for a moment before moving on. "Any other vehicles we can send out?" He pauses, waits. "Anything. Bicycles? There are settlements not more than five or six miles away. Anyone be willing to walk out to Cedarcrest? Maybe the Francis-Mark Forebay?"

One of the guys raises his hand. "I got a brother over in Francis-Mark. It's a walk, but I'd be willing to head out there. They're all holed up in and around the chapel, last thing I heard. I think there's some boys from the old militia out there too. Might know where we can get more guns."

"Good." Jeff again. I close my eyes, rub at them. They're still trying to fight this whole thing like a ground war and I don't have any better ideas. I look over at Stoff, see that he's wincing again, near tears. "More guns and more ammo. Anyone else have any ideas?"

"What about the bunker out on the North Fork river canyon?" One of the guys asks. "That one that space-alien cult built in the old Indian caves?"

"I've heard of it." Jeff watches the guy with an even stare. "Always thought it was an urban legend though. What about it?"

"Well, I heard they stockpiled all kinds of stuff out there. Military stuff." He looks at a couple of the other guys in the pause. "Grenades and shit."

"Think you can get there?" Jeff asks him point blank, catches the guy off guard.

"Uh, yeah, I – uh..." The guy hesitates, looks around at the others. "It's only about six miles up the road, out Grizzly Mine, if I remember correctly. Never actually been there."

"It's worth a look," Jeff says, gestures. "Take three guys with you. Go armed in case someone used that bunker for something more than just a weapons cache, and don't take any stupid risks." He pauses, looks at me, lets his eyes move across other eyes. "We've lost enough people already today."

"We've still got some cleaning chemicals in the shed up by the kitchen-house." Another har adds, attracting eyes. "Some odds and ends, old copper pipe fittings, spare nails, that kind of thing. Could probably rig up some real basic bombs with help from Bryan." He makes a gesture, indicates another har, a guy dressed in nothing but overalls. "Won't be as good as those grenades you mentioned." He looks at the har who brought up the bunker. "But they'll be better than nothing if you can't find the place or if it's already been cleaned out."

"Every little bit helps." Jeff nods, turns to Stoff. "Stoff. Any ideas?" Nothing. No response. Jeff looks at him, blinks, and I can see concern spreading through his features, his eyes. Stoff wipes at the moisture around his own eyes, sniffs, shakes his head.

He's a mess, a wreck. I cross to his side, sit beside him, reach up, massage the hair and skin where his scalp meets his neck. Only one or two guys look away, embarrassed by the affection in the gesture. In the pause, Jeff crosses his arms, looks at me. "Tyse?"

What can I say? *There's a way to set them on fire by touching them?* That's worse than suggesting that we jump out of a ditch and stab them with spears – and it'll sound twice as crazy to everyone around us. Better to just go with the *armed defense* plan for a day or so, then bug out in the middle of the night, head east, take Stoff with me. With a little luck, we can fall in with a pack of Varrs in the next state over, or maybe keep moving until we hit the other coast. There are a lot of dangers out that way, I've heard, but nothing sounds more dangerous right now than the *things* that took Cinder Hill.

"Stoff needs rest," I offer. It sounds hollow, but Jeff nods anyway, lets us go.

"Keep thinking," he says, and I nod in return.

Once we're outside the bunkhouse, I stop Stoff, take a moment to look him over, make sure he isn't hurt. He's pale, deathly pale, and sweating, shaking, but I find no blood, no open wounds, nothing.

"Are you hurt?" I ask him, and he shakes his head. "What is it, Stoff?" I push. "What's wrong?"

The look he gives me is so full of pain that it hurts me to meet his eyes. Lips tremble at the edges of words, struggle to get them out. "The voices," he says. "Ever since – ever since that flash, something's different – in my head. Something's changed. Something – there are *voices.*" He tries, but the words stick in his throat again. In the pause, I take him in my arms, hug him, hold him.

"Voices," Stoff says, shudders, sobs openly. "They're getting louder, Tyse. They're so loud, and they're getting louder all the time."

CHAPTER 17

Stoff's words, his admission scares me a little. Voices? I ask him what they're saying, but he just shakes his head. He looks sick, damn sick. I take him to the barn, set him up in a cool, dark corner with some water, then rush off to the kitchen-house. No one's around, so I rifle through the cabinets and the shelves in the root cellar until I find some dried goat stock. It isn't much, but it might help, I figure. It's a hot day, and there's a makeshift solar oven at one end of the property, so I fix him up a bowl of soup, pilfer a few crusts of acorn bread to go with it, take it all back to him.

He's asleep when I get back, so I soak one of the crusts in the soup and eat it myself, leave the rest with the bowl on a nearby shelf. He looks better, now that he's asleep, I decide, and after a while, the heat of the day and the weight of the bread in my belly start to wear me down. The ranch is quiet by the time I curl up next to Stoff. Most everyone is gone, all off on orders from Jeff, but here and there I hear someone shout or go running past the barn. It isn't enough to stir me. None of the shouts sound too urgent, too frightened. *Just a little nap,* I tell myself. *Been a long day already. Just a little nap.*

When I wake, I wake with a start. It's dark, completely dark, and the night is dead silent. I wait, coming to slowly, just listening, parsing silence for even the sounds of crickets–

And then I hear it, loud and strong, maybe a few hundred feet away.

The call of a mountain lion.

"She knows," Stoff says, and suddenly I'm aware of him, of the way he's sitting up beside me, staring into the night beyond the deeper darkness of the barn. My lips part on the edges of words, can't seem to find anything to say. Stoff's voice comes again: "she hears the voices too."

There's a moment of silence, and then I hear the mountain lion call out again. She doesn't sound any closer, any further. It's almost like she's in the same spot, like she's *waiting*.

"She wants us to follow her," Stoff says. I swallow, reach out, touch the naked skin of his back. He isn't sweating anymore. His flesh doesn't feel clammy. I feel him turn, flinch a little when he touches my cheek.

"How do you know?" I finally find the strength to ask, to whisper.

"The voices," he says. "They're so loud now, Tyse, but I'm learning to control them. I'm learning how to listen to them."

"What do they say?" The words tumble out, breathless.

Stoff's hand leaves my cheek. Fingers trace lines down my chest, then rise, disappear into the darkness.

"They say that there is something in the woods that we have to meet. There is a voice in the darkness that has all of the answers."

And then he gets up. I hear his footsteps on the dry dirt of the barn floor, see his silhouette black against the stars in the sky as he reaches the door. The mountain lion calls again, and when Stoff moves, I push myself out of the makeshift bed, fall on hands and knees, scrabble with pants and shoes, stumble to catch up with him.

"Stoff!" I yell. It's hard to see him – the stars, the sliver of the moon, there's only so much light, and he's hauling ass, moving at a dead run. I stumble over something, trip, hit the dirt, come up again and throw myself after him. Can't let him get away. Can't let him run off into the woods alone.

And then, just as suddenly, he stops.

We're maybe ten feet from the trees at the eastern edge of the ranch. I almost run into him, stumble and reach for him, but he catches me before I fall, holds me. The first thing I notice is the tremor in his arms. He's shaking, just a little. The second thing I notice is the *breathing*.

It comes quiet at first, like a snort, and so close. Maybe five or ten feet ahead of us. My eyes search the darkness, but I already know what it is, what's there in the night with us.

And then she calls out again, the cougar, and the sound is so loud that makes all the hair stand up on end across my body, turns my stomach to ice. I don't move. I'm fucking paralyzed by the sound. It brings back so many memories, so many terrifying tales I was told as a kid about mountain lions falling on joggers, stalking friends and relatives through the brush, their eyes always hungry, their claws always sharp, so sharp.

That call comes, and this time it sounds even closer. I can feel her in the darkness– or maybe I only imagine I can. I cling to Stoff like a frightened child. There's nothing to do – run, and she'll kill us. Move toward her, make threatening gestures, and she'll kill us. She probably weighs as much as one of us, could probably maul us both, drag one of us off, leave the other to die.

"Show us," Stoff says suddenly, and I can tell he's not talking to me. He's talking to *her*, to the mountain lion.

"Stoff," I try, but he hushes me. In the night, I hear a quiet, rattling growl. God, she must be close enough to touch. I pull at his clothes, but he only holds me still, stands as rigid as a board.

"We're ready." Stoff says, and his voice is terrifyingly steady. "Show us."

Another sound, something like a wet snarl, and then I hear her turn, hear big, padding feet on pine needles. Crazy as hell, Stoff starts to *walk forward,* lifts me and drags me with him. I'm too fucking scared not to follow, not to walk with him into the woods.

I don't know how long we walk, how far. At some point, I hear leaves and brush rattle, scatter as the cougar rushes ahead of us, stops, calls out in the darkness. Holding me, all but carrying me, Stoff pushes on, moves faster. He's strong, so strong, seems to be getting stronger the deeper we go into the woods. The mountain lion calls again, and then we're almost running. Branches whip past, slap us, cut us, and still we run.

And then, suddenly, there's a light in the darkness. The mountain lion shouts into the night, but the sound is further off to our left now, seems to be receding as she trots off into the thick, abyssal forest. The light is small at first, a will-o-wisp floating maybe twenty feet off the ground, drifting lazily through the trees. Stoff slows, then stops suddenly.

And then I hear it, so close it brings the terror right back full force. A howl, a rattling yell that's unlike anything I've ever heard before in the woods, and it's maybe six feet from us, off to the right and behind. Stoff doesn't even turn. It's like he knows it's there before it even announces itself.

Breath catches in my throat – another howl answers the first, just as loud, just as ferocious-sounding, and off to the left somewhere. Then another, ahead. Then a fourth, until the whole darkened forest is alive with alien voices screaming hateful sound through night, through trees.

And then the light flares suddenly, blasts us with spotlight violence, blinds us from above. There's a sound, but I can't place it, can't make sense of it. Pine and cedar whip in the air as if stirred from above by the blades of a great helicopter, but none of the rotor-noise is there. Instead, there's only a deep, vibrating hum that seems to roll over and through everything. It's not loud, but still it drowns out the screaming, drowns out all thought until all we can do is stare.

All at once, I feel Stoff break away from me. I don't fight it – I'm paralyzed, but not with fear. With something else, something I can't describe. I'm terrified, sure, but there's a *force* holding me in place, keeping my feet rooted even while Stoff steps forward, walks into the light, becomes one with it, disappears when it all ends suddenly, *completely.*

It's like someone flips a switch, kills the power entirely. The sound, the light, the screaming, the trees – it all ends instantaneously. In the silence that follows, I stagger, stumble, listen but hear *nothing.* "Stoff!" I call out, get no answer. I listen again, listen harder, but there's nothing, no sound, no movement, *nothing.*

"Stoff!" I try again. After a moment, I hear a mountain lion call out in the distance – just once, quickly. Maybe it's the same one we followed. Maybe, but if it is, she's gotta be a mile away by now, further, probably.

I don't know how long I stay there, how long I wait, listen. I call for Stoff until I'm hoarse, but no one ever answers. The light, the screams – they never come again. Eventually, the crickets pick up, fill the silence, and that's when I start to feel alone, *truly* alone.

I don't remember falling asleep, but I wake when dawn comes. The air is cool, the first light soft and blue. There's spit hanging from my lip, pine needles caked against the side of my face. I push myself up slowly, dazed and lost, look around, recognize nothing.

"I know what they are," Stoff says, and I turn quickly to look at him, find him sitting cross-legged on the ground, his eyes so clear, so calm. He's looking at me, looking into me, and as I shift on the mat of decomposing deadfall, he looks away again, looks to the patches of morning sky visible amongst the trees. "They aren't aliens," he says. "They're machines. They're machines that man built, designed with our destruction in mind."

"How – how do you know?" I ask, half-lost, bewildered.

"I met *him,* Tyse." He looks back at me, and his eyes are spooky, catlike. "The first of our kind. The *Aghama.*" I swallow. It's a word, a name I've never heard before. "I met him, and he told me *everything.*"

For a moment, I can't speak, can only stare. When words finally start to coalesce, before I can ask any of the questions bubbling up inside me, Stoff smiles softly, reaches out for me, touches my face.

"I can't explain it. Let me *show* you," he says, and then he's close to me, so close. There's a confidence to him that makes my lips tremble, and then the touch turns into a caress. He looks at me with those eyes, those eyes that seem like they really have seen *everything,* whatever that all is, and it leaves me breathless. Doesn't matter. When we kiss, he gives me his – *his breath,* and it's *alive,* colorful, full of images, sounds that black out the day, replace reality with something else, with something he can only share through the sweat of his skin, the touch of his flesh, the heat of his exhale.

And as he presses me down into the soft bed of dirt and detritus below me, I leave my body – or at least, that's how it feels. I go somewhere else, and yet even as I watch our bodies melt, merge to become one knot of soft, stirring flesh, I know his spirit, his soul is with me on the other side. I feel his hand, his presence, let him guide me into something else, some other shade of reality, some fragment of memory washed with the light of another world, another phase of being.

Let me show you everything, Tyse.

Let me show you what we are, what we are meant to be.

CHAPTER 18

When I was a boy, I fell off the roof of the house. My dad and his friends thought it was funny as shit, laughed while I lay there crying and twitching. Didn't break nothing – I think that's why they didn't get up to help me, hold me, check me over, but at the time it felt like a betrayal. "Don't go into the light, boy!" I remember someone yelled. "Lordy me, don't go into the light now, ya hear me!?"

Don't go into the light. I didn't get the meaning then, the reference, but it's one of those things you pick up while just living, without looking for it. Later on, I'd hear those words – don't go into the light, and I'd think about that fall, about the ground rushing up to meet me, about the betrayal of drunk relatives braying with sick and spitting laughter over the misfortune of a child.

Don't go into the light.

The place that Stoff carries me into is all light. It's nothing but light. It's white, brilliant, clear, not blinding, not painful, but brighter than the brightest day I've ever seen. It's pure. It's exactly the opposite of that moment I remember. There's no pain, no sadistic laughter. It's like being submerged in the cool waters of a silent ocean, floating in liquid void without needing to breathe. In the moment, I don't want to be anywhere else but in this light.

Stoff moves. I'm conscious of it somehow, don't see it, don't feel it, just *know* it. Colors come out of the pale, run like veins through light as they brighten, all prismatic, alive. Like thin rivers, they run together, become something else, become memories, the face of a man – no, a *har*. I can't see him, not really, but the colors cut his edges from the light, steam from him like silhouettes of rainbow fire as he steps toward me, offers me a hand.

Aghama, I know, and it's like I'm reading someone else's memories. It's like my mind is larger, like my soul suddenly has access to more brain than it usually does. The word rises from the light, takes on meaning. *The first one. The first har.*

Memories. A flash of concrete walls, steel-grate flooring. I see a child prodded with needles. I see men with paper masks talking about dire things that come muffled, too indistinct to hear. I see the world crack apart and fall, rise again reborn, covered with hara, but it's all symbolic, all transition translated into imagery only half seen. It's his credentials, I realize. It's what he remembers. It's the birth of our species, the history of how we began, how we became what we are now, the key to something *more*.

"We are all equals," he says, and his voice sounds as soft as silk, as strong as the distant rumble of thunder. "We all walk different roads, but the result of awakening is the same."

Awakening. New images flash through my mind, new concepts. *Realization.* Hara that move *between* layers of reality. Hara that shed their skins and become light, turn that light into flesh anew. Hara that are whole, neither male nor female, not even both, but something *new*, something wholly separate from human, something I've felt lurking inside me for as long as I've been har. Something like wings restrained by the codes of a cocoon I wove myself with years of repetition, habits, fears. Something that *aches* to get out.

And it's so easy to set it free, I see now.

"It isn't just a *state*," the Aghama says. "Look deeper."

Deeper. It doesn't come as a word, veiled and meaningless. It comes as concept, colorful, ringed with memories. I see the frames, understand, go *deeper.*

The mind. A greater mind. A mind with its fingers in countless other minds. In the moment, I see pieces of other lives. I see a Varr who lords over a massive manor. I see the children he sires. I see their children. I see bits of what they see, what they do. I see countless others. Uigenna, Unneah, Colurastes, Kakkahaar. I see tribes that have no names for themselves yet. I see tribes I shouldn't know, would have no way of hearing about, no way of knowing the names that others have made for them. I see their minds, their memories, but only in flashes. The experience is merciful that way – it's all glimpses. It's all paint, a gloss that doesn't stick, that carries me toward *understanding.*

And amidst it all, I see my life, my memories, and Stoff's as well. I see his mind, understand him, see the pivotal points in our friendship, our *relationship* from both sides. The clarity is incredible, yet so little of it is retained. Only what's most important stays. I see the Aghama, the subtle ways he pinched and tweaked the fabric of reality to create certain junctures, to assure our lives continued instead of ending suddenly. He knows the future for Stoff, for myself, I can feel that. He's been guiding us ever so gently, leading us toward something he won't show either of us yet – or at least, *won't show me.*

"You have a powerful purpose. You have a role in this world," the Aghama says. "Both of you are needed if Wraeththu are to survive. Both of you are needed to put an end to the threat that took Cinder Hill, that killed so many, will kill so many more if you do not act, and soon."

"What are they?" I ask.

"Machines," he says. "Machines built by machines and controlled like a singular body by a machine mind."

Images. Gold Country, the hollow hills rolling, soaring underneath me as if I were an eagle. Beneath me, the smoking ruin of Cinder Hill rises up, and I see the gutted buildings, the mechanical activity in the street. Beyond the eyes, I see so much more. I see the web of electromagnetic chatter that rises and falls through the streets, connects everything into a single network run by a single mind. The signal comes from a building I recognize, the radio station a block or two south of the Cinder Hill Inn.

When I go deeper, I understand. Images of a man come to me, a man with flat, rectangular glasses. His sleeves are stained with black grease, his busy fingers tapping out code on the plastic keys of a shining laptop. I see the seeds of the machine mind coming together, the lines of protocol that guide it even now. It's so simple, I realize. Painfully simple. Linear. One dimensional, yet powerful in its focus. Its goal, its purpose, is malicious, steeped in hate. I see a teenager, a boy kidnapped by scarred and tattooed Uigenna, dragged away from a father with flat, rectangular glasses. I see the boy's body on a street corner three days later, hollow and half-har, skin cracked and blackened, corrupted by a failed inception. I see the father's pain, his hate. I see his mind, so strong, so brilliant. I see it bent by the vision of his son, corrupted into a myopic hatred. I see the two months of labor that follow, the child of hate he births, teaches to hate us as he hates us.

The rest comes in shorter flashes. A hijacked satellite. A

clandestine upload. Fear, adrenaline. Hands on a steering wheel. A food riot in the streets. An overturned car. Flat, rectangular glasses broken and bloody, kicked by an unconscious foot stumbling across pavement. I see the machine mind as it gathers itself, as it plans, as it adjusts the course of its frail body until it is stronger, thick with the corpses of other satellites. I see it create for itself a body like a meteorite, see it adjust its orbit until it slips into the atmosphere, falls right where it knows it will be seen. One purpose burns in the mind of the thing as I watch myself wrap the winch around it.

Cleanse the Earth of hara. Only hara.

"It watched us, studied us for a long time before acting," the Aghama says. "It saw the Rift of the Damned as the best place to begin its conquest. It saw the resources, the sparse population, the buried and forgotten military research facilities full of equipment it could put to use. It saw the potential for an easy start and a chance to build an unstoppable army." He pauses, fills me with images of darkened corridors flickering with light, mechanical arms working with a ceaseless rhythm, creating, constructing, fitting masks of black glass onto dark, steel bodies. One after another. One after another after another until there are dozens, hundreds, *thousands.* "There is only one way to kill it now that it is here, only one way to save our kind. You must take Stoff to the heart of the thing. You must get him to the fallen star. His touch, his awakened mind is the only weapon you will need."

The radio station. I see it in perfect clarity, see inside it, see the thick cables that bind the mess of servers the machine mind has made into its brain. In the midst of it all, the meteorite is there – shining, full of precise holes that hang with heavy wires. *There.* I know, and yet I have no idea how it's possible. The streets of Cinder Hill are thick with the machine's drones, every one of them with a built-in rifle, with targeting software precise enough to put a round between the eyes of anyone unlucky enough or dumb enough to get within a quarter of a mile. A full-on assault is suicide – that much is obvious, but something else, some other way. . .

"Stoff knows. Stoff sees it. He sees the holes in the perfect web the machine thinks it weaves." *There's a way in, a way through,* I realize. "Follow Stoff. Listen to him. Trust him as your body has learned to. It will take both of you to end this threat." I feel the Aghama's stare as he seems to look into me, seems to study me, regard me with eyes that search through the stuff of my soul. "Remember this," he says. "Remember what I have said. Remember all of it. Remember it even when you find yourself wading through the dead."

There's a flash of something there, an image leaking from the mind, the soul of the Aghama, but I can't catch it, can't see anything more than the blur of a stricken face, a mouth hanging open, full of flies. It's horrifying, but here in the light, there's a peace to everything I see, feel, take in and understand.

"Awaken," the Aghama says, and we do. We come back as if borne by a river, carried by a stream of light to the peak of orgasm, the apex of connection. In Stoff's eyes I see an echo of understanding. He knows everything I know and more. His lips part, my hands tighten across his sides, and then there's a warmth, a heat, the sweetness of relief. He doesn't collapse on me as he has in the past. He's spent, I can tell, but he's different now, more aware of himself, his body. In the silence that follows, we breathe together, share sweet kisses, gentle caresses. I feel more myself than I ever have before, feel like I've passed a milestone, blossomed in some important way. If I had wings, they would be outstretched, flexing feathers toward the wind. I want to fly. I want to be fully har. I want to awaken more of myself, and as I see my need, my passion mirrored in Stoff's eyes, I push him over playfully, press him into the softness of the forest floor, ride the wave of our tangled bodies as they shift, take on new roles, become liquid *together.*

And as I slide deeper and deeper into his being, become one with him, with his skin, his soul, his eyes, I feel like the parts of me I've kept too long restrained are finally bursting free, breaking bonds forged with human code, human ideas. With Stoff, I soar. *We soar,* rise together, let the winds and the sky and the sounds of life surround us, burn us to nothing but light – and still we continue to soar, scatter our own ashes on the wind.

When we come back to our bodies, we are sweat-slicked and breathless. Still, I lean in, kiss him, share my passion with him, share the heat that stirs like a living thing in my breath. In the distance, we hear a mountain lion cry out, scream to the newborn day, and it makes us laugh, smile. His eyes are so beautiful, green brown, an echo of earth and leaves. He reaches up, brushes cool sweat from my forehead, collects the buds of happy tears slicking the edges of my eyes.

"This is what it means to be har," he says to me then. "Remember this, Tyse. Remember me like this."

"You'll always be beautiful," I smile back, kiss him again, feel him rise into my lips, into my chest. "I love you, Stoff," I add in the breaths that come desperate between kisses. "I love you. I love you. *I love you.*"

CHAPTER 19

There's no way to tell how much time has passed. It feels like an instant, is thick with enough memories, sensations and moments of bliss to fill a thousand years. Smiling, drunk on sweat, on the feeling of liberation, of rebirth, we wander out of the woods with clothes hanging loose, with new rips in our shirts, new stains from rolling in the wet dirt. Pine needles crunch and spring underfoot as we wander back, vaguely following some memory of last night's run.

When we reach the edge of the woods, wander down a slight, rolling incline of goat-mowed grass and cross into the peach orchard, something pulls me back, pulls me away from the moment, away from Stoff. There's a smell to the air – acrid, lingering. The orchard is eerily still and quiet. Ripe fruit lies scattered across the path, peaches dropped and bruised, some already starting to rot. I look ahead, see nothing but the buildings of Segerstrom Ranch, look back to Stoff, but his eyes don't look over, don't meet mine. There's something grim about his features, suddenly. His eyes – they look haunted, and again I get the feeling that he knows more than I do. Much more.

We come across the first corpse just beyond the orchard. I recognize the guy, but can't place his name. Stoff only glances at him, keeps walking. I can't help but linger. The way he's lying, the skin on his face sallow and stretched, showing teeth in a disturbing scream, his mouth open, full of flies – it's the same face I caught during my time with the Aghama. It's the same face he tried to hide from me. It's a piece of yesterday's future reflected into the present.

"Tyse," Stoff calls for me quietly. I look up, realize I've been staring at the corpse for a long, lingering moment. Other bodies lie here and there, all so precisely executed, every one of them silenced with a single bullet to the brain. Some are bloated, look like they've spent days in the hot sun.

"How long were we gone?" I ask, step over another corpse, another guy I recognize, one pale hand still tight around the grip of a pistol. I've seen so much death, somehow knew this was coming, somehow knew that the hara of Segerstrom Ranch would never be prepared enough to face the machine mind's deadly drones. There's a feeling of something like peace seeing it done, knowing it's over, knowing there's nothing anyone can do, never was anything anyone could do.

"A day or two," Stoff says. His steps come even, neither hurried or slowed by the bodies of our friends, the hara who took us in. I follow him, swallow, keep my eyes on him until he crosses to the back door of the bunkhouse, moves inside.

It takes my eyes a moment to adjust to the darkness as I stop inside the doorway, blink. Movement leads me to Stoff, and as I step forward, I notice he's crouching next to something – a corpse, maybe.

And then it moves.

"Stoff," I take a step forward. He doesn't say anything. The corpse twitches only for a moment, rubbery fingers juddering, flexing, finally seizing. Getting closer, I see what he's doing – one of the *things*, one of the machine mind's drones is lying in one of the concrete doorways, burnt and blasted, glass-plate face shattered and stained with dried darkness. The gun-arm is outstretched, its last shot clear. Beyond the door, collapsed against the wall, I see Jeff's eyes, empty of life, of spark. A clean shot to the forehead, just like all of the others. I look away, close my eyes.

"What happened?" It's all I can manage.

"Last stand," Stoff says. I catch the movements of his shoulders out of the corner of my eye. As he works, I stare at the floor, the wall, anything that offers a trace of normalcy. "The machines hit the ranch while we were gone. Almost everyone was here. They're all dead now." He yanks something from the drone, stands, breathes. I swallow, turn, look at the mass of wires, plastic and chrome sitting in the palm of his grimy hand. He looks up at me, his expression blank, unreadable. "They never knew it, but they gave their lives so that we could live."

I look at Jeff again, at the shotgun in his hands. The damage to the drone is unmistakable this close. Point black range, enough buckshot to shatter the glass, open the machine for Stoff's hands, almost as if it were planned that way.

"Come on," Stoff says, turns to leave.

"Wait," I try, hesitate when he stops, turns back to look at me. "Shouldn't we. . . shouldn't we bury them?"

"There isn't time," he says, and it comes so simply, so matter of fact in tone. I look away, and in the pause, he slips back into the light, leaves me alone in the bunkhouse.

Again, I look at Jeff, days dead, try to remember what he was like when he was alive. Try to remember what his smile looked like, the color of his living eyes, the way his dreadlocks hung when he had them hanging loose about his shoulders. So much death. So much.

Goodbye, Jeff. My lips part a little, but I don't breathe the words. It's cowardice, maybe. I don't know. I turn back to the door, squeeze eyes against the hot buds of fresh tears as I step forward, follow Stoff.

Outside, it's already getting hot. I look up toward the hills to the west, the dead grass shining, golden. Somewhere not too far away, a goat calls out, hungry. Chickens look out from the wire mesh windows of their coop, already panting, wide-eyed and scared. They've been locked inside since it happened, locked up with no food, no water. I feel sorry for them, slip the lock on the hatch that leads into their coop, let the flock pour into the yard. The smell of rot reaches me. Broken eggs, the flattened bodies of one or two of the birds who didn't make it through the last day or so.

I look up as the chickens pick over the ground at my feet, hear the sound of cans and bottles clinking together coming from the open door of the kitchen-house. Stoff gathering supplies, probably. I look around the ranch, wonder if I'll ever come back here again, if anyone will ever come back here again.

There's time, I decide. It only takes a few minutes to unlock all the gates, let all of the livestock into the yard. Another few minutes to walk to the barn, roll back a barrel with six months worth of sweet feed in it. The animals don't wait – the instant I have the lid off, they're all over the barrel. All I can do is rotate it, let the stuff pour out on the ground. They'll go through it all in a week, if it takes them that long, but it's better than nothing.

"Tyse." I look up, see Stoff standing in the doorway of the kitchen-house. He's got a woven hemp sack slung under one arm, heavy with food, with jars and glass bottles. "Time to go."

I nod, don't say anything. Stepping over the chickens desperately gorging themselves on feed, I run my fingers through the coarse fur of a preoccupied goat. I try not to think about what will happen when the chickens find the corpses in the yard, what will happen when the predators in the woods realize that the ranchers are gone.

Stoff crosses to the road that curves through the ranch, waits for me. When I reach him, he starts north, follows the road as it meanders toward the bunkhouse and the barricaded exit beyond it. Only when we've left the ranch do I ask, "where are we going?"

"Cedarcrest," he says. In my mind, I know it's only a handful of miles up the road, but nestled in a tree-crowded cleft in the first heights of the stony eastern mountains, it feels like we're making a pilgrimage to the top of the world. There's a settlement there, I know. A lake. Almost as an afterthought, Stoff adds, "Everyone there's dead too."

I close my eyes then, slow. Stoff doesn't wait for me, just trudges on across the asphalt at a steady speed. He doesn't even look back. Lost, I watch him shrink, approach a corner where I'll lose him if I don't move, and suddenly I'm hurrying again, eyes wet at the edges with fresh tears. I can't lose him. Not now. Not when the world is like this, upside down, full of death.

"The machines hit every major settlement in a fifty mile radius from Cinder Hill," Stoff says when I finally catch up to him again. "Jimtown, Nephilcamp, Coluton, Francis-Mark, the guys out on New Milo Lake. They're all gone. They're all dead."

"How do you know?" I ask, but I already know. It's denial that makes me ask. Stoff only looks back, smiles softly at me. *He knows,* I realize. *Of course he knows.*

The day is hot, gets hotter, but the further up the hill we hike, the more gusts we get, the more air there is blowing down from the icy peaks to the east. The road out of Segerstrom Ranch leads as much north as it does east, finally connects up with a four-lane highway that I know goes over the pass and into the next state. *We could run,* I think, but it's only for a moment. We can't run. Not from something like this.

"Only a few more miles," Stoff says, kills the thoughts. I look ahead, squint east. Cedar and pine a hundred feet tall or more rise on either side of the highway, make a wall more symbolic than substantial. Stoff cracks open a bottle of that sweet dogwood berry wine, takes a swig, passes it to me, but I only nurse it. Even the goat cheese and acorn bread we share sits like lead in my stomach, doesn't seem to nourish.

When we reach the off ramp for Cedarcrest, it almost comes too sudden. All the signs I'd follow on the road when I was younger, when I was human are gone. Not even the creosote-treated posts are left to mark where they were. The ramp looks right, though, looks familiar. Stoff doesn't even hesitate, seems almost guided by some other sense as he descends into the trees, crosses an intersection, makes his way into the lakeside resort village turned har settlement that is Cedarcrest.

The first bodies come into view maybe a few hundred feet from the highway. A snarl of traffic clogged with corpses, all dispatched as simply, as easily as all the others. No need to check any of the vehicles. I can tell even as we pass that they've all been disabled with the same precision. The road cuts in toward the cold, stony lake, cuts across flat, paved ground that's all open, gray and cloudless sky above with trees and mountains crowding in around us from every direction. Cedarcrest feels like a bowl, a bowl full of boarded-up buildings, the ruins of rusted cars and the stink of ripening corpses.

When Stoff leaves the road, I keep following him. The corpses seem to thicken around the old post office, a brick building scarred by fire and time. Lots of guns, lots of rifles clutched in bloated, sallow hands. Lots of faces with snarling mouths, blind eyes staring out of bloodstained flannel, orange-brimmed hunter hats. Some of the rifles almost look like they'd be worth braving the smell for, but Stoff hurries past, doesn't leave me time to prise any of them from cold, dead fingers.

"How much further," I ask, but Stoff doesn't say anything, just points at a skinny green signpost with an orange snowpole sticking out of the top of it. *Granite Ln.* Doesn't ring a bell, doesn't look like a road I've ever taken. The lake disappears behind a wall of pine and cedar as we descend down a shallow incline to a cold, one-lane road cloaked in the shadows of towering trees.

Maybe a mile. That's probably about how far we follow Granite Lane. Houses peek out of the richly green, almost malachite-colored foliage that crowds so thick around the road. No scrub this far up. No manzanita, no dry grass, and oaks are sparse. Just incense cedar, sugarpine and ponderosa pine. Here and there, we hear chickens, but we never see them. Whether they're penned up, locked in coops or free, I can't say. I try not to think about it.

It's getting late when Stoff leaves the lane, crunches out onto a gravel driveway and descends another hill. I look up, look vaguely west, but the trees are too thick and I can't see the sun. No way to tell how much time we have before the night comes, but the chill in the air is familiar. Won't be long now. Maybe an hour.

The drive is short, just steep enough for the gravel to be slippery. At the bottom, a house sits against the edge of a flat lot like a toddler at a table, sags on legs that barely keep it suspended there. It reminds me a little of the canyon houses in Blackjack, more of that impractical architecture favored by the rich. Stoff sets down his sack, walks right up to the garage door, grabs handles and rolls the thing up into the ceiling. Inside, there's a tangle of black metal. He walks to it, crouches down, goes to work.

I stop maybe a hundred feet from the house, glance at him, glance at the sky, the road. Another drone, I figure. Another last stand. I've had my fill of corpses for the day, for the year, hell for the rest of my life. When Stoff stands again, gestures for me to come over, I almost ignore him, actually linger for a moment, but something gets me moving again, brings my feet to the dark and yawning garage.

"We have what we need," Stoff says, crosses out of the garage, pulls the door shut again. For the brief instant I can see inside, I catch only the glint of light across steel, something that looks like an engine on an orange engine stand. No bodies, and I'm grateful for it. Stoff smiles almost like he can read my mind, holds up another mass of plastic cut with chrome, hanging with wires. "Now all we have to do is consecrate them." He stuffs the thing in the sack, shoulders it, then walks past me again, still smiling. "Come on," he urges again, crunching his way back up the drive toward Granite Lane. "Let's go get dinner."

CHAPTER 20

Dinner.

It's dusk when we reach the center of town, the road that curves along the lakeshore and passes all the primo rental cabins and snack shacks from the days when Cedarcrest actually had tourists. The crickets are already out, already singing with the approach of night, and the sky mixes red-blue in a tight band at the rocky horizon. One of the larger lodges on the shore turns out to be an inn as we get closer, a restaurant with rooms upstairs that was still in use until the attack that left so many corpses spilled in the street. The door of the inn is locked, but a window gives Stoff and I a way in. No bodies inside, but plenty of food in the kitchen and a fireplace stacked with dry, seasoned wood that keeps the cold night at bay.

It's pitch-dark by the time Stoff and I get settled at a table, share a bowl of day-old chowder made from buckeye and freshwater clams that's a little heavy on the salt. While he heats up the chowder, I gather a dozen tallow candles from a closet, light them, put them around the main dining room, get the fire started. The whole place lights up well – the wood furniture is all polished and lacquered to a shining, almost ridiculous degree, so everything reflects the flames, keeps the heat.

The chowder and the fire keep us warm, but the cold descends quick, and soon we're shivering in our T-shirts and jeans. I make a trip upstairs while Stoff rummages through the kitchen again, looking for more stuff to eat.

The doors to the rooms are open, unlocked. They look lived in, like they were once the rooms for a bed and breakfast, but recently have been the sanctuary of the lodge's owner, maybe the help as well. Hard to tell. No bodies, but there's plenty of warm clothing. I pull a couple of fleece jackets from a worn-out gym sack in a corner, tug one on, bring the other down to Stoff. By the time I reach the dining room, he's back at our chosen table again, knife in one hand, something dark and leathery-looking in the other.

"Whatcha find?" I ask.

"Duke avocado," he says, holds it up, grins for a moment before sinking the blade into the skin. He makes quick work of the fruit, exposes the creamy green interior easily, flips the pit out onto the table. I trade him one of the jackets for half of the avocado, pick up a spoon and rub some of the grime off of it.

Stoff doesn't dig into his half immediately. After the fleece comes on, he pulls the salt and pepper shakers from the nearby windowsill, dashes a little of each across the green flesh of the fruit. His spoon goes in easily, and he eats the thing with the same shit-eating grin that kids wear when they're eating ice cream. It's fun to watch. I take his cue and put a little salt and pepper on mine too. Even as old and dusty as the spices are, they make the avocado taste damn delicious.

"How far out do you think this came from?" I ask him between bites.

He smiles at me, and I can tell he's really savoring every spoonful, letting the meat dissolve in his mouth, working it apart with his tongue. "Not far," he says, points with his spoon. "These are a frost-resistant cultivar. Could have come from a tree pretty much anywhere west of the snowline."

I nod, take my time with my own bites. Even with the

hot weather just a handful of miles west, avocados are rare in the Gold Country. Most of the working orchards were in the Valley-That-Was, and the few trees I've seen are rare enough, far enough from each other that they never seem to fruit. I can count on one hand the number of times I've seen avocados at the Sunday market. Sometimes it seems like gasoline is less scarce.

When Stoff finally scrapes the last bit of green out of the avocado skin, he sets it aside like a trophy, puts the pit inside the open curve almost as if doing so comes as an afterthought. I finish mine not long after, put the skin with his, smile as he drags out more of that sweet dogwood berry wine, takes a slug, passes it to me.

The night passes like that. Food and wine, snatches of conversation. It almost feels normal, almost feels like the world hasn't gone crazy just outside the door of the inn. At some point, I ask him about the components, about his plan, regret it when his smile falls a little in response.

"Right," he says, and the room is too quiet in the pause. I can't help but swallow, look away. When he finally speaks again, it's only after he stands, crosses the room, then turns back to face me again.

"Come here," he says.

I blink, watch him for a moment. The smile comes back a little and he gestures, encouraging me to follow as he starts toward the stairs. I'm the only one of the two of us who's ever been up there, and yet, for a brief moment, it seems almost like he knows more about what's in the rooms on the second floor than I do.

Another gesture. When he's almost to the top of the stairs, I pry my ass loose from the chair, cross the creaking wooden floor to the staircase, look up. It's so dark up there with all the light flickering through the main dining area, but I can still see Stoff's shape in the frame where stairs open into the hallway above. Or at least I think I can. I blink, and then suddenly the shape is gone.

Steps give a little, squeak and groan as I climb them. When I get near the top, I see a flash of light, see Stoff's face in the glow from a cigarette lighter. He looks at me, smiles, gestures, turns away.

I see enough before the light goes out again to find my way into the room where Stoff is poking around, tossing things through darkness. It's not the same room that the fleece jackets came from – it's messier, full of canvas sacks and greasy clothes. It isn't long before he turns back to me, hands me what feels like a heavy aluminum toolbox, goes back to digging. I lift the thing a little, but I can't see anything in the crowded darkness, so I carry it out, bring it to the bottom of the stairs. By the time I return, Stoff's found whatever else he was digging for, meets me in the hallway briefly, then hurries past me, back down to the dining area.

I hear the metal clank of tools against the inside of the box as he lifts it, carries everything over to our table, pushes aside the leavings of dinner. Besides the toolbox, the other thing turns out to be a beat-up tackle box with a green body and a brown lid. In the light, I can see the peeling stickers on the side of the toolbox, some of them colorful, others flashing silver. They're all for old racing parts brands I'm vaguely familiar with, mostly companies that went out of business long before the collapse, if I remember correctly. The hard grease caked into the creases on the box is another indicator of its age – decades old. Thirty, forty years, maybe.

Lids come open and I watch as Stoff roots through the

tools, pulls out a pair of pliers, a thin, metal file, an old stitching awl with a polished oak handle and a length of tin solder. The tackle box turns out to be full of beads, spools of what look like quilting thread, buttons and other odds and ends. I look over it all for a long moment, then look up at Stoff, search his face as he paws through the bottom of the tackle box, pulls out a length of beaded chain.

"Anything I can help with, Stoff?" I ask.

"Not yet." He looks up at me, smiles. The chain he sets aside, gathers into a pile, but the awl, the file, the pliers and the tin solder he keeps separate.

I watch as he strips off his jacket, his shirt, takes the tools and the tin to the fireplace, then uses the iron poker on the rack beside it to rearrange the logs. When he's finished, there's a hot little hollow between chunks of wood, the spot just big enough for him to heat the tip of the awl in. The chunks of plastic and wire and chrome from the drones come out of jean pockets next, and then I get what he's doing. A length of the tin solder sits softening by the fire. Amateur electronics. Campfire soldering. Something I never saw or thought would actually work until the world fell apart.

It takes a long time. The process is slow, has to be precise. The tip of the awl can never come in contact with the ashes or the wood, and periodically he has to stop to scrape the carbon from the steel with an old butter knife. The pliers give him the leverage he needs to pop loose pieces, pieces he resolders elsewhere. Eventually, he has me bring him what's left of a roll of electrical tape, makes loops of the exposed wires that knot one into another like some kind of crazy Viking design. When he's done with the first, he sets it gently to the side, and all I can say is that it's neat-looking. I feel on some level like I should know what it does, almost recognize something in it, in the way the lines of solder dance together in such delicate designs, but when it comes right down to it, I really don't have any idea what he's made.

"I'm making one for each of us," he says as he starts to work on the other one. Every drop of liquid solder falls so precisely, is shaped so carefully by the glowing-hot point of the awl. It's mesmerizing to watch Stoff work, to watch his hands manipulate his tools so carefully, so fluidly.

"What do they do?" I ask, watch as he draws a thin line of boiling tin across plastic as if it were ink and the awl were a calligraphy pen.

"They're talismans," he says, leaves it at that. The awl goes back in the fire for a moment, starts to glow as he glances back at me. "When they're done, they'll get us into Cinder Hill."

Cinder Hill. I look at the thing as he goes back to work on it, lick my lips. *Talismans?* I think of the chunks of pottery a kid I knew in school used to wear on necklaces, chunks of pottery he called *talismans.* Weird magic Indian witch voodoo shit, and yet– and yet there's something there. In the case of Stoff's talismans, I know there's something there, even if I can't place it. I watch, wait until he's done soldering the second one, done knotting up and taping the exposed wires, then ask the only question I can.

"How–" I start, hesitate. "How do they work?"

"They don't," he responds, grins out of one side of his face. "Not yet." He turns back to them briefly, turns the second one over in his hands. "These are just the material elements of something... of something *larger.*"

I have no idea what he's talking about, and yet

somehow there's a memory, or a piece of a memory that resonates with his words. Part of me knows exactly how it all works, but that fraction of my soul is still all mist, is full of dream sounds that linger like so much half-heard Spanish in the ear of a Gold Country gringo like me.

Stoff looks at me again, sees the confusion on my face and smiles anew, softer this time. "Here," he says, turns, holds out the drone-chunk he's been working on. "This thing – it's like the brain, or maybe the seat of the closest thing these guys have to a consciousness or a soul." He turns it over in his hand again, shows me the exposed circuitry. "The machine mind is like the collective unconscious which moves through the unifying layers of life-spirit. It's neither part of it or wholly disconnected from the underlying *us*. It's like a facet of a world soul that speaks a wholly different mind language..."

He trails off, bites his lip in the pause. It's clear from his face that he only half understands it all himself, that the concepts mating and meshing in his mind are gifts from the Aghama, a foundation of alien ideas that fit together as easily as an eighth dimensional screw and screwdriver might, if you lived in an eighth dimensional world. Here in three dimensions though, it's all just gibberish, medical Latin in the hands of an American grammar school boy.

"Way I understand it," Stoff begins again, looks back to the thing in his hands. "The electric stuff has memories, uh – *computer code* in it. We just have to stick part of our soul in the circuitry so we can use them, so we can *know* how to speak the language they share, how to blend in, be seen on some level as *one of them.*"

"And you know how to do all that." It comes more as a hopeful statement than a question.

He nods immediately. "The Aghama showed me how to consecrate them, how to, uh, link them up with our souls." He pauses, exhales nervously, glances back at the talisman sitting on the stones beside the hearth. "It's. . . *new*," he hesitates, breathes, shakes his head. "It's all here, but it's also so new. He's laid out the instructions in my mind and I'm getting better at understanding him." He looks back at me. "All of this is weird, Tyse, but it all makes sense too." He picks up the two talismans, stands, turns to me. "We can do this. I can do this with your help."

"Whatever you need me to do," I say, watch him as he glances back to the fire, the tools lying on the stones at his feet.

"Okay," he finally says, looks back at me, meets my eyes. "Take off your clothes. I need you naked for this to work."

CHAPTER 21

This is what it means to be har.

Stoff's words from the morning come back to me as he slips the long length of beaded chain over my head, lets the talisman come to rest in the center of my chest. I look at him, look into his wide, aware eyes, look at his lean, toned arms, his smooth, almost silken skin. *Weird. New. Wonderful.* All words to describe how he looks, how I feel, how it feels to be har. In the pause, he reaches out, touches me lightly on the arm. When he raises his hands to chest level, I understand, raise my own, press my palms against his.

"Close your eyes," he says, and before I do, I see him do it first, smile a little, just an edge. Behind him, the fire crackles and roars with the last of the cut wood, puts enough warmth into the room to bring sweat to my skin.

"Aghama." The name leaves his lips with a trace of tremble. Together, we wait, listen, *feel.* "Aghama," he says again, this time with more force, more conviction. When he says it the third time, I put the name into the air with him, intertwine my voice with his. "Aghama!"

Suddenly there's an electric resonance in the air. It rolls into us in the silence, builds, hums through the skin, stirs strong in the vault of the chest. I can feel it through Stoff's palms. I can feel it in the talisman I wear. For a moment, I almost open my eyes to see if anything's changed, but Stoff seems to know my thoughts somehow, breathes, "Don't, Tyse. *Trust.* I need you to be *here*, now."

I am. I let myself slide into the moment, stand like a steel rod, feeling like lightning might strike at any instant.

"Aghama," Stoff whispers again, and as the last syllable passes into air, I feel that presence again, that streaming heat, that haze of prismatic light. "Welcome," I hear Stoff breathe, and I echo him almost immediately. He's here. The Aghama is here. Some part of him is in us, *with us,* moving though and between us. Reality feels suddenly porous, fluid, permeable. There's a smile, but I can't say whether it's mine, Stoff's, the Aghama's or all of us smiling at once. "We are one," Stoff says, and I feel it in that moment. I feel present, *connected.*

That's when the ideas, the sense-image concepts come flooding through me. It's like he's guiding me, like we're all guiding me with one singular hand, one tide of flowing soul. I become aware of the talisman at my chest, and suddenly it feels like a living thing, like a creature, small and silent, waiting. No one speaks, but I understand what I have to do. I understand how it all *works.*

There's a point in my chest, a spinning, fiery green vortex filled with light, with color. I see it, feel its wild heat just beneath the plastic of the talisman. *That's where the touch must come from,* I realize. It's hard at first. It's all so new, so weird. With hands that aren't hands, I siphon a little of the fire from the vortex in my chest, lead a tendril of it to the talisman, feed it into the lines and wires there.

Weird, but it makes sense, somehow. The tin and silver lines are like nerves, neurons, but simpler, crude and limited in their capacity to hold soul. It's simple to *possess* the thing, to integrate with it as if it were a part of my body, but I can also see how easy it would be to burn the whole thing out. It's so fragile, so small inside that I feel like a giant inside a tiny paper house. Only when we all move together again do I see the complexity the talisman holds, the key to getting into Cinder Hill.

Another step back, another moment of feeling too large, too clumsy. It takes me a moment to refine the fire I'm pouring into the thing, to realize that I'm forcing it to play by my rules, forcing it to accommodate me instead of stopping, listening, *learning*. When the awakening comes, I wait, explore the thing with just the barest, needle-thin edge of soul, learn it the way a blind man learns a labyrinth.

And that's when I start to pick up the language.

It's all just impressions at first. Hazy shades made from points of void and light. There's a hierarchy to it all that doesn't make sense at first, and then I realize how *linear* it is. Simplicity – that's what it is. The whole thing is so simple, too simple. On and off, that's it. Complex constructions composed entirely of dots, of *ons* and *offs*.

Once I understand the foundation of the language, everything else starts to make sense, starts to fall into place. Bricks of ons and offs combine into buildings, into glyphs the size of skyscrapers. The glyphs have meaning by themselves, but together they can create words, express greater concepts, more complex ideas. It's a language, totally different from anything I've ever experienced in my life, but being inside it, exploring it with the purest essence of mind, of soul, I pick it up quick, absorb it completely.

And that's when Stoff, or the Aghama, or all three of us – that's when we discover the *library*.

That's all I can think of to call it. If the talisman is a labyrinth, then the library is its center, the brain within the brain. The whole outer area of the labyrinth is powered by code that can be skimmed, understood simply by watching it move, but the library itself is dense and silent. It's like an oracle that the rest of the talisman consults when it needs advice, needs to know codes and protocol outside those of normal operating procedure. To understand it, I have to get inside it, have to take it apart and *wear it*, learn everything it knows.

Codes. So many codes. I take them all, gather them. There's a code that says *I am one of you*, another code which gets that code to a satellite in orbit, and another code for a second satellite when the first is out of range. There's a code that says *I am functioning at optimal efficiency*, and a code that says *I am busy performing another task*. They're like hats, signs, keys. They unlock doors, answer questions, appear to function passively, even when they are anything but. Learning them all, translating them across the breach from machine to meat isn't necessary – they're all there, in the talisman, in the library. I just have to look them up, send them with the part of my soul I keep there.

I open my eyes then. Stoff is looking at me, right at me, and in the pause we both seem to reel a little with the sensations of learning how to use a second brain at the same time as our first. There are things it can do, transmission protocols – there's so much, and it's all there now. It's all part of us. Meeting the queries of the machine mind come easy, as easily as lifting an arm, wiggling a toe. Simultaneously, we both test it, feel the codes as they fly, connect with satellites, communicate with the network. It's instantaneous, and yet as it happens, time seems to slow. We're aware of every step, aware of each other, aware of how the central mind perceives us. It doesn't seem overly concerned when our signatures pop into the network, doesn't even send a query for an explanation. Most of its units are on standby for the night, conserving power until they're needed, and the focus of the mind is elsewhere. Even a flag for assistance might not be noticed, it seems so preoccupied.

"It's so simple," Stoff says as we drop out of the network, take off our talismans. I'm conscious of the thing even when I'm not wearing it, but I feel lighter without it. Weird sensations, like something from a dream. I look at him, blink. "The mind," he adds. "The *machine mind.*"

I nod. "Seemed that way to me too." Its focus was sharp, razor quick, and yet it seemed so *limited*, like it could only look at one thing at a time.

"We're lucky." Stoff sets his talisman aside, pauses a moment to look at it. "If it was more advanced, if the guy who programmed it had taken more time to develop it, getting close would be a lot harder. It'd be looking for irregularities instead of actively ignoring anything that doesn't reach out and touch its mind directly."

"So these are all we need?" I look at my own talisman, study it for a moment.

"Yeah." Stoff nods. "They'll get us inside the perimeter the machine mind has built for itself, keep us invisible to it at least until we get to the radio station - I think." He pauses, shrugs. "The closer we get to the star, the more likely it is to notice us, but we have to take that risk. We can't wait for it to get any stronger or kill any more of our kind."

"Yeah." I know he's right, feel some trace of the Aghama in his words, but really thinking about it all makes me nervous as hell. "How do we stop it when we get there?" I look up at him again, catch his eyes. "Just tear out a bunch of wires? Trash everything electronic inside the radio station?"

"You remember what happened on the railroad

tracks?" he asks.

"For the rest of my life." It brings the traces of a scared smile to my lips.

"I'm going to do *that*," he says, his own smile showing, spreading, "only this time, *I'm going to do it to the star.*"

Chapter 22

We sleep in the dining room that night, gather quilts and blankets from the rooms upstairs and build a nest a handful of feet from the fire. What's left of the firewood we supplement with pieces of furniture, chunks of kitchen shelves we break up with hammers. Stoff arranges it all for a slower, cooler burn, and then we make love, right there in the middle of the dining room floor, wrapped in a layered cocoon of cool sheets and cooler sweat.

When it starts, it starts soft, almost innocent. Caresses, eyes lost in eyes – it feels familiar, feels right. It isn't the frantic fucking of a couple's first time together, but it isn't passionless either. It's kind, it's patient. It's confident, serene. We trade roles fluidly, rise and fall together, delight in the bodies we share with one another. I love his curves, the way his skin catches the light as he rides me, throws his head back, the glistening heat between his thighs taking me, caressing me. I love the way he stretches me when he mounts me, the way our legs become a tangle of feet and ankles when we're looking into each others' eyes. I love the way he grips the blankets with one hand, his wrist rigid against my side, his free fingers sweeping up under the curve of my ass, gripping me, guiding me as he fucks me. It's hot, so hot, and when I feel myself open for him, open in a way I never have before, I ride it, *go with it.* We both do.

It's like cumming, but stronger somehow. I feel him moving, some part of him darting deeper, like an eager tongue teasing the slick walls around it. On some level, I know what it wants, what we both want, but I'm blind to it. In the moment, I just want it, whatever it is. There's no thought. The approach to it feels amazing. I look into his eyes and I can see the need I feel mirrored there as he slides deeper, as the heat between us builds toward some kind of higher peak, some transcendental explosion of spirit and –

That's when it happens. Some part of him lashes itself to some blinding button somewhere inside me, paralyzes me while my hips rise into his, take every inch of him as deeply as possible. I'm open, so open, gone while he shudders, while he howls and bares his teeth with the wave of release washing through him. When I come back, I can't speak. Almost can't breathe. My whole body feels like it's made of light, like my skin is a shell of pleasure around a void that's finally been filled. His hands grip my ass desperately, and then he falls forward into me, kisses me back to consciousness.

"What– ?" It doesn't all come out at once. I'm still quivering when he pulls out, when the melange of our sex juices runs from the petals of the blossom between my thighs. Even coming down from – from whatever it was, I still feel it, still feel the wash of orgasm, the breathless relief. He grins into my cheeks, reaches up, caresses my face, kisses my forehead. "Stoff," I try again. "What was that?"

"A gift," he breathes, buries his face in my hair, takes in my scent. "Something the Aghama taught me. Another lesson in what it means to be har."

The words are like sweet nothings; they pass without sticking. I wrap my arms around him as he breathes through my sweat, then I kiss his shoulder, his arm. When he rises again, his trembling lips find mine for a moment, share his heat, his breath with me, liquefy whatever parts of me might still be rigid. In the moment, I'm his completely. I'd do anything for him. *Anything.*

And then he props himself up between my legs, smiles at me with one of those big grins I love. "Sleep, Tyse," he says, and it makes me giggle a little. Innocent, pure. That's how I feel. Completely safe, insulated from everything by the moment we share.

Strong arms hold me as we shift onto our sides, wrap ourselves in each other, let our arms and legs become comforting knots of skin on skin. We sleep like that for most of the night, and only once do I wake up, notice that the fire has died down to embers, to nothing but coals among ashes.

Morning comes slow, comes cold. Blue light filters in through windows that look out on nothing but walls of endless cedar, verdant pine. Stoff's already awake when I come to, and I notice the way he's staring into the coming day. His eyes are patient, calm, as if he's accepted whatever is meant to happen between now and nightfall, as if he's completely at peace with it all. Sympathetic, almost wistful, hopeful, I reach out for him, pull his warmth closer, and the gesture brings him back. He pulls in a long, deep breath, then turns to look at me, smiles, lifts my hand and kisses it softly.

We only linger a little while. The crisp coldness of the air feels good, and while Stoff dresses, I cross into the kitchen, naked as the day I was born, root through the cabinets that are left until I find breakfast.

There isn't much in the kitchen that isn't canned or moldy, but I do find some treats that sound good to start the morning with. A dried out custard of some kind, flavored with boiled toyon berries. There's a sourness to it that tells me it's going south, but it's still pretty sweet, brings a little brightness to our morning, to the solemnity of what we're about to try to do. Slices of green apple come on a plate on the side. Big pieces – still sour, not yet ripe, they make a nice counterpoint to the custard, leave us feeling lighter even as we wash it all down with the last of the sweet dogwood berry wine.

Doesn't take long to gather up everything we need. "No guns," Stoff says. "Nothing that could be recognized as a threat." It makes me nervous, the idea of going right into the den of the beast without any firepower on our side, but then I think of Jeff, of all the guys piled up outside of the Cedarcrest post office with neat, even holes in their snarling heads. Guns didn't do any of them any good. Better to trust Stoff, tuck in my fear, move on.

We stuff the hemp bag with what we can. No tin, no pop-tops, nothing metal or glass. We pour all the clean water we can find into a pair of old ceramic whiskey jugs, plug them with kitchen rags. All the metal buttons, everything the machine mind might be interested in, we get rid of. I cut the zippers off our fleece jackets, poke holes in the fabric so we can lace them up with nylon twine. It does the trick, isn't the most comfortable thing in the world, but will be more comfortable than wearing t-shirts while the day's still cool.

The talismans come on last, slip down under our shirts. Following the memories of last night, we close our eyes, reach into them, log in to the network. Still no query from the mind in charge of it all. There are thousands of points in its network all performing different critical tasks. A couple of units coming back online unexpectedly at the edge of its range doesn't rank highly enough to be worth looking into.

When we leave the lodge, I mentally calculate the distance from Cedarcrest to Cinder Hill. Thirty miles or so, maybe a little more. Hell of a walk, especially if we're planning on some kind of siege at the end of all of it. Turns out Stoff has something different in mind – a truck, but not all the way into town. Just to a spot maybe a quarter mile short of where the machine mind's signals start to get thick. Some memory, some idea from the Aghama guides him to a vehicle that still runs, still has a couple gallons of fuel in it.

It's enough. Stoff puts the pedal down, gets us to a shopping center about four miles outside of town. When we ditch the truck, I look up toward the sun, squint. Ten o'clock. Maybe eleven.

The Eighty-Eight cuts a sweeping line toward Cinder Hill that the machine has been using like an artery to send its troops out to the settlements and ranches further east. Walking down the highway keeps our steady, inward march from being suspicious. The road's empty when we cross it, eerie and silent. Not a single car, truck, bike or body in sight. "It's eaten them all," Stoff says as if reading my mind. I look over at him and he looks back, swallows, looks back to the road ahead of us again.

I swear I feel it when we cross through the perimeter. Mentally, I'm aware of it through the link the talisman has with the network, and with every step I half expect the great eye of the machine mind to come sweeping our way, interrogate us, strip us down with digital queries and drone inspections until it's clear we're not part of the hive mind. Minutes pass. It doesn't happen. We move into the outskirts of Cinder Hill unmolested. None of the guys with the guns or the black, glossy planes shows up to shoot at us, bomb us, even look at us. Stoff breathes a quiet sigh of relief as the highway dips down and the first buildings beyond the last rise come into view. *Yeah*, I think. *I feel it too.*

"First test," Stoff says, smiles.

And now I'm nervous again.

The closer we get to the center of town, the more hollow things seem to get, the more the stores and homes start to look like facades, like flimsy shells. Most of the buildings still standing in Cinder Hill are brick, concrete or stone, but they're *empty*, look almost like the skeletal remains of the civilization that built them. Wooden shacks, streetside homes and shops bolted together or made from leaning pieces of corrugated metal against walls are all just nests of garbage now. The machines have taken everything, *everything*. They've pulled the windows out, stripped the plastic from everything, sucked out all the bolts and wires and melted them down to make more drones.

But there aren't any drones. None that we can see, at least. Even main street is empty. Not a single glass-masked face in sight.

"Where are they?" I lean toward Stoff, whisper. It's weird. You'd think that the brain, the lair of something as dangerous as the machine mind we've come to kill would be swarming with drones, but it isn't. Here and there, the road shows cracks, scorch marks – all that's left of a battle, but there are no corpses, no lost weapons, no soldiers standing silent vigil. Every footstep echoes through the dead town – and then the rusty tower of the radio station comes into view, rises over everything like a demonic horn, twisted and orange.

"They're here," Stoff says, and the words come so quiet I almost don't hear them. *They're here.* I look around, but not quickly, not searching. My movements are stiff, terrified. The open doors and windows of buildings crouched along main street yawn back at me, impenetrably dark – and then I realize that darkness could hide anything. Could hide drones.

Part of my mind is in the network. Stoff's right – I can see them through the talisman. Five or six in every building, just waiting, *waiting.* There are countless others elsewhere, slaughtering hara in settlements to the north and south, but there's also an impressive amount of the fuckers right here in town with us, close enough to come alive and put a bullet in both of us before we could even turn or run, before we could even flinch. It's unnerving, puts my teeth on edge. "Just keep moving," Stoff whispers. Right. Three blocks to the radio station. Three blocks until it all ends, one way or another.

Three blocks.

Keep moving.

Chapter 23

I'm surprised when we reach the front door of the building. Pleasantly surprised, but there's no sigh of relief, no release of the tension building in my back, my shoulders. One look at the two story building, at the first floor that's completely filled in with solid concrete and the upper-level outer windows that are plated over with three-inch-thick sheets of steel tells me all I need to know. This is where things get hard. This is where we win or where we die.

"What do we do?" I breathe. The radio station looks impenetrable. The only staircase is on the inside, locked somewhere in that mass of concrete. I look up again, look back at Stoff. "Knock?"

"There has to be a way in," he whispers back, eyes crawling all over the barricaded front. Through the talisman, I can tell that he's scouring the network at the same time, unobtrusively tracking patterns, trying to find the traces of a route to the star we both know is inside. "It wouldn't be smart for it to just lock itself away from the world. If some important part blows, it'll need a way to get replacements inside. There's probably a way for drones to get in. . ." He pauses, pulls in a deep breath, wipes sweat from his forehead. "We just gotta find it."

"What about a back door?" I ask. I know there's a lane that runs along behind the buildings on main –

Suddenly, there's gunfire. Two shots, *zwip-zwip*. I hurl myself at Stoff, jam him into the crack between the sidewalk and the outer wall of the radio station, cover him with my body, only open my eyes when I realize the network is still sitting silent. No alarms, no queries.

The machine mind hasn't even looked up from whatever task it's working through.

Beneath me, Stoff is panting, scared. He looks up at me, eyes darting across my face. He looks as surprised as I am that we're still alive, that neither of us is bleeding, that the whole mass of sleeping signals around us hasn't swarmed into the street, intent on crushing us. In the silence, I help him back to his feet, check his shirt, his arms and legs as he looks past me, searches for something out of place, for a gun, a corpse, the traces of fired rounds.

"I thought," he tries, looks further up the road. "I thought I heard–"

"Yep," I cut him off quickly. *Totally untouched.* I look across the street, check the storefronts, look north, opposite direction from the way we came in. *Nothing.* "Bullets," I say, shake my head. "But they weren't meant for us."

Stoff turns back to me, studies my face again, trying to make sense of what just happened. "The network didn't even flinch. It sounded like one of the drones, but nothing *woke up.*"

"I know." I meet his eyes. The shots were so quiet, so quick. Close, but neither of us can figure out where they came from. I look at the hollow stores across the street again. *Nothing.*

"Come on," Stoff says, moves past me. "Let's get this over with."

I follow him as he makes his way north, steps lightly, carefully, glances across the street and up the road with cautious eyes. There's no easy way around or up – small town blocks aren't like big city blocks. They aren't even, aren't regular. We walk a few hundred feet before we find a way across to the lane that runs parallel to main, follow that back south, back toward the radio station.

Every building we pass seems to have either a second storefront or a blank back wall facing the lane. All the hinges, bolts and everything else metal are gone – all that's left are more hollow eyes and yawning mouths full of silent, sleeping death. I try not to look at them, try to keep my eyes on the road we're following. In my mind, I turn over the moment when the shots came cutting through the air, turn it over and over, trying to figure out where they might have come from, who they might have been intended for.

Doesn't take long before I find out.

The lane that goes behind the radio station doesn't cut straight south. It veers a little toward the west, rises, ripples and bends in the subtle ways that old gold rush roads do even decades after they've been leveled and paved. By the time it reaches the radio station, it's fifty yards from the back of the building's second level, rising up and curving in to dump itself into the northwest corner of a simple little ten-car lot.

The first things I notice are the bodies scattered across the lot. None of them are human or har, and some of them are days old, but a few look fresh, the blood still wet and pooling. *Squirrels*, I realize. Squirrels, rats, pigeons, feral cats. All dead. All lured in by the pair of chokecherry trees dying in planters just a handful of feet from the back side of the radio station. All precisely silenced the instant they had the misfortune of wandering into the car lot.

And that's when I see the drone.

I stop instantly, grab Stoff, point. The drone is silent, still, stands against the only door into the radio station. The back door, second level. Stoff looks at me, licks his lips.

"I know how this works," he says. I look at him, try to figure out what he means. "The Aghama," he adds. "It just came to the surface. It's been there all along, but I–" He hesitates, shakes his head.

"Talk to me, Stoff." I whisper back.

"That drone... He points. "There's a reason why the whole network stayed silent when it fired off a shot. It's set up that way on purpose. It's like a bouncer. It guards the door, puts rounds through anything moving that crosses into the parking lot, doesn't trouble the main mind with the details."

"Okay." I look at the drone again. "So how do we get past it?"

"It won't fire on an active friendly signature," Stoff says, still looking at the drone, turning back to me when he adds: "We just go right up and knock, like you said."

"You're joking."

"Yeah, kind of."

I look back at him again. "What're our options?"

"Only one option," he says. "I've seen it. We're going to walk right up to that drone and I'm going to set him on fire, kill him in one hit." He pauses, swallows, glances back at the drone for just an instant. "The whole hornet's nest is going to come alive then. We're gonna have about fifteen seconds before this lot will be swarming with the fuckers."

"Better hope the door isn't locked," I shoot back.

"It is," Stoff says, smiles. "But the drone's got the key built into his wrist."

"You're fucking crazy, Stoff." I grin, shake my head.

"Yeah." He smiles a little wider. "Kiss for luck?"

I don't answer, just grab him, press him into the

nearest wall and shove myself against him. The kiss is long, desperate, leaves him gasping, dazed. "It'll work," he says, then says it again between panting breaths, almost as if he's trying to convince himself, instead of just me. "It'll work. I've seen it. We can do this. It'll work. I've seen it."

"I trust you," I say, kiss him again. I don't trust the visions, the knowledge, not completely, but after everything, after all the Aghama has shown him, all the times Stoff seemed to otherwise divine the locations of dead drones, that working truck, food – I know that I should, that I owe at least that much to him. We have to try this. I have to follow him. *Both of you are needed,* I can hear the Aghama say, and for a moment, just a brief moment, I almost feel like it's more than just a memory of something he said, almost feel like I caught it on the wind instead.

Stoff kisses me again, brings me back to the moment, but the heat, the passion has passed. We break away a little, and as I hold him, Stoff looks away, glances at the ground, the road. When he looks back, he seems happy again, just slightly, and I can't help but smile.

"Come on," he says. "Let's do this."

He doesn't give me time to answer. Quick, smooth as a cat, he slips out of my arms, crosses back to the edge of the lot and just stands there, watching the drone. When he looks back at me, I cross the distance between us, stand with him, feel like I should say something, but there's nothing to say, nothing to do but take that first step.

Stoff pulls in a deep breath, looks up at the sky. We take the step together, then the next, then the next. At some point, I look over at the drone, but it doesn't react,

E. S. Wynn

doesn't look up. There's no twitch to the gun-hand, no flash, no blood. I look back at Stoff, see how serious his face is. He doesn't look back.

The closer we get to the door, the more the corpses start to thin. The smell is sickly sweet, the sun-ripened rot of road carrion hanging heavy in the air, almost tangible. Here and there, buzzards, other scavengers drawn by the smell lie silent amongst the others, and suddenly the whole scene fills me with a sense of sadness. A cat, a little dog – some Chihuahua mix, probably. Some of these animals were probably once pets, once loved. They deserve better than this. They all deserve better than this.

So many bodies that deserve to be mourned, to be buried.

Stoff keeps moving, doesn't stop until he's almost close enough to touch the drone. In the silence, he looks back at me, doesn't say anything. I get the meaning. I nod.

And that's when all hell breaks loose.

I'm maybe eight feet from the door. Stoff pulls in a breath, then closes the distance between himself and the drone in a single striding step. His hands touch steel immediately, one palm coming up flat against the glass mask, the other seizing the metal wrist that holds the key to the door. There's a flash, a spike of heat, a gust of wind that stirs his hair, and then the drone is moving, *alive*. It's terrifying – I can't move, can't do anything but watch. Steel squeals, and then the drone takes a staggering step toward Stoff, falls. The key comes free from the glowing steel with supernatural ease – then Stoff turns, tosses it to me.

And then the eye, the full attention of the machine mind – I feel it shift toward us, feel the queries that hammer our talismans. Even before I can catch the key, the machine mind figures out our cheap disguise, knows who we are, *what we are*. Stoff tears the talisman from his neck, tosses it to the ground. I don't wait – I immediately jam the key into the door, turn it, feel the deadbolt clunk free.

And the instant the door comes open, I feel the sleeping drones of Cinder Hill wake up. I feel all of them wake up, come alive, swarm out of hollow stores and into the light. *Fifteen seconds,* I remember. *Fifteen seconds.*

Yeah, I think, half-tracking the signals in the instant before the machine mind reaches into my talisman, locks me out of the network.

If we're lucky, we'll get fifteen seconds.

CHAPTER 24

I throw the door open, catch the inside handle. Stoff is past me in the space of a breath, rushing into darkness as I hop-step backwards, pull the door closed again. My hand goes to the lock, stops when Stoff calls out – "leave it. Won't slow them down any."

I turn back, but he's already gone, already lost somewhere in the jungle of heavy cables snaking through the shadows. The only light comes from the chunks of computer hardware wired together into massive, junky towers. Everything has an odd, blue glow – and it's cold, like being inside a refrigerator.

"Stoff!" I call out, step over a bundle of cables, try to put some space between myself and the door.

"Here," he answers, and the word comes quick, gives me a direction. I stumble almost immediately, fumble over cables –

And then I see it, see the star, polished and shining in a glowing cradle of wires and chattering plastic. Exactly how it looked in the vision, in the dream – all studded with cables, like a heart, like some crazy sci-fi nightmare on late night TV.

Stoff steps forward. That's when I see him, catch the silhouette of his shape as he reaches for the star. There's fire in his hands, a glow that glitters off chrome. I step over a bundle of wires, don't even flinch as the door explodes somewhere in the darkness, throws a sweep of light across the towers. *Seconds.* Stoff doesn't look up. His hands go flat against the star, throw heat into the steel. *Seconds.*

Zwip-zwip.

My hands go immediately to my chest. No pain, but then I see the way Stoff bends in the sparse light, the way he folds up at the middle, almost falls. One hand still grips the star, and as the other goes to his chest, I see the fire in the chrome get brighter, flare through the meteorite, send cables flying, flashing with electric light.

"Get down!" Stoff yells. There's blood in his voice, a wetness. I don't listen, I just stand, stare. Something moves quick and heavy through the darkness, but I don't care, don't even look up when it falls before reaching me. At my chest, the talisman flickers with soul, comes alive again.

And then I hear *the screaming.*

It's the machine mind. Stoff's burning it out from within, slaughtering it in the digital realm. There's fire all across the network, fire, hazy readings and standby warnings as dozens of drones shut down and collapse under Stoff's unflinching assault. I see his teeth bared in the half-light, in the shadows, see his eyes, see the slickness of blood running down from his shirt, soaking his pants. He looks at me –

I can't do anything else. I run to him. I want to stop him, drag him out into the light and look at him, yank the bullets out of him and scream the Aghama's name until some miracle of healing comes flashing from the sky, and yet I know it's not meant to be. I know there are limits to everyone's power, that there are times and places like this, like now, that require sacrifice. I can't stop him, and he knows he can't stop. He knows he has to do this. When I reach him, I look into his eyes, and I can see that he's known for a long time that this is how everything comes together. He's known since that first vision, since those first voices broke into his mind after the flash at the railroad tracks. He's known all along. *He's known.*

"Tyse," he says, grabs me, leans into me for support. "It's looking for another satellite. It's looking for a way to upload itself so it can come down again somewhere else, start all this shit over again." There's a clank in the doorway as the pile of dead drones gets so thick it blocks off the light. I blink. The shadows on his paling face are twisting, red as blood.

"What do you need me to do?" I ask.

"Help me," he says, can't keep the building blood from bubbling over the rim of his lips.

"How?"

"Like this," he says.

I can't stop him, hardly realize what's going on until it's done. His hand is on my talisman, his soul is mixing with mine. Fire flares behind my eyes, and then I know – it hurts, but I know. I get what he's doing. The concepts burn, flash chaotic, but I get how it works, how the translation of one electric force to another will put me face to face with the machine mind.

"Go," he says, and the word means so much more in the moment. His eyes flutter, but I'm already gone. I'm already somewhere else.

There's a moment of vague awareness. Both hands hit the glowing steel, fingers splayed, palms burning with a fire that's all drive and no heat. In an instant, I'm in the network, the light of my being riding the wake of codes the talisman offers up like a second, lightning quick brain. It's like flying through space, and the eye of the machine mind is like a sun, a star under siege. It's blinding, and every point of light caught in its orbit is a drone with orders, with purpose. Stoff has shut down so many of them. The mind is in pain, near death. I watch as it reaches into its own library of codes, searches for options, for ways out faster than any human mind could track.

But I'm not human, not any more. I'm har. I'm a spirit unbound by flesh, alive in the digital by force of will alone.

Eleven satellites. It checks each one, drops five as unsuitable, marks three as emergency options. They're all too small– the machine mind doesn't want to cram itself back into a tiny box. It wants to find a way out that will give it all the processing power it needs to run things from orbit, give it room to expand. Only one satellite it looks at seems to have enough data capacity to make it viable – and then I realize that the other two satellites aren't ways out. They're *threats*.

The machine mind doesn't speak to me, doesn't implicitly tell me they're threats, but I can see it, know it immediately. Both are old orbital weapons platforms. Nuke sats. I access them even as the machine mind tries to shut me out. I'm inside just long enough to see that the coordinates are locked on Cinder Hill – and then a code-prompt closes off my access, leaves me with only one satellite to look at.

The machine mind triggers an upload, sets a very visible tripwire of code between itself and me. The message is simple. *Let me go.* If I cross it, if I kill the mind before it can upload, even try to crack the linkage between it and the nuke sats, the whole town, hell, all of the Gold Country, every square mile of the hollow hills will disappear under a mushroom cloud the size of Utah. There won't be anything left. Manticker will feel it up in Duwamish.

I only hesitate for a moment, but it feels like an hour.

The upload ticks along, hits forty percent. *Can't let it end like this,* I decide.

Five minutes. That's the only warning I get when the nuke sats light up in the network, both bright red. Part of me tracks them while they prime their aging missiles, prepare to pound the Rift of the Damned until it's nothing more than a big crater of radioactive ash. The machine mind is terrified, and it should be. I am har. This is the only chance I'm going to get to end this, to wipe out this threat to our kind. Damn the missiles. Damn the Gold Country.

Time to be a fucking hero.

There's a scream, something like a scream as I reach into the coding for the upload and tear the machine mind in half. Wipe protocols fired off quick as bullets eviscerate the data on the satellite, leave nothing but the chunk of the mind that's still here on Earth. Suddenly unbalanced, it tries desperately to defend itself with only half its senses intact, becomes as spiky as a pincushion, folds in on itself in an attempt to hide its wounds, protect the broken code leaking off into the digital ether. It isn't enough. It's no match for my rage, the raw spirit of Wraeththu surging through the hands I use to shred it. In seconds, it's dead, disintegrating in digital space like a ship torn apart by a storm. Flotsam, jetsam. Nothing more.

Silent, empty, I come back. The star is silent in the network, now just a cloud of fractured code and flashing dust. The last of the drones collapse trying to tear their way into the radio station, and I watch them as their little quasi-minds wink out one by one. The only things still active are the nuke sats, and as I sit back, I realize what I've done. They're both locked up tight, secured with passwords I can't even fathom how to break. Every time I try to get close, they drop my connection, knock me back into the ground-based network. Two minutes tick by. Three.

Make your peace, I think. I can tell from looking at them that their missiles are almost ready for launch, are sitting up there in space, points aimed right at me, at the center of Cinder Hill. In another minute or so, engines will flare, carry them to me, to the Gold Country. In another minute or so, nothing else will matter.

Tyse.

On some level of being, I open my eyes. There's a connection in the network, weak, but present, like an echo of a signal. I query it, get only the code for a typographic grin back in response.

And then I realize – *Stoff.*

Half in the network, half out, I turn my head, look at my lover. He's almost gone, but he's grinning, still has one hand on the meteorite. I try to speak, but nothing comes – and then I realize where he is, what he's doing.

There's a piece of code he puts out like a key, uses to secure a connection first to one nuke sat, then the other. I watch in awe – it's so fluid the way he does it, his movements so confident, so smooth. The code-key slides into algorithmic locks, turns both satellites from red to green. Countdowns freeze at fifteen seconds, reset, and then both sats shutdown, *forever.*

Unplugging from the network feels like falling. In the darkness, I fumble for Stoff, find bloodslick hands, follow them to his face. "Stoff," I try, but there's no answer. His lips are cold, still hold the traces of a smile. Tears pull at the edges of my eyes, break and run.

"Stoff!" I shake him. Nothing. I reach up, hold his

cheeks, try to kiss him, but he doesn't move, doesn't kiss back. The cables around us are like the rubbery tendrils of some giant dead horror, seem almost to swallow him in the darkness. Screaming – I think that's the sound that tears itself from my lungs. Tears – thick, hot, endless. Tears and screaming. Desperate kissing, the tearing of hands at clothes. Blood everywhere.

A day passes like that, I think. Feels like a day. Feels like more. No way to know for sure with all the drones blocking off the doorway. I don't want to face what's left. I don't want to live without Stoff. So many dead bodies, so many dead people. It's like the chaos of a few years ago all over again, and this time I don't want to live through it. I want to die. I want to be with Stoff. I want all this shit to end.

But it doesn't end. The endless night goes on and on and Stoff's body gets colder and stiffer. It makes me sick, being that close to him, being that close to the waxy husk that's all that remains of him. I've got no reason to leave, but I know that if I stay, it still won't end. I'm meant to live for some reason. I'm meant to live and I hate it.

Eventually, the hate fades. The pain is still there, but it dulls with time, becomes an ache that keeps my eyes teary more often than dry. I feel hollow losing Stoff, but something else rises to fill that space in me. Something new. Something out of place. Something bright. Something almost *hopeful*.

It doesn't make sense, but it's enough. At some point, I say my final goodbyes to Stoff, turn to the herculean task of dragging drones out of the doorway, opening the dead radio station to the world again. It takes a long time, seems to take forever, but eventually I get out into the light. The first thing I see is the mass of corpses on the pavement, the bodies littering the parking lot, but this time they aren't the corpses of cats, dogs, squirrels and birds. They're the corpses of drones, of glass-masked machine men like those that killed Stoff, that killed Jeff, Bill, Yuri, Davy, Ray, Hima and countless others. Like a sea of monstrous scales, plated mannequins of black steel and heavy plastic, they stretch on and on as far as the eye can see. Thousands of them. *Thousands.*

All felled by one har.

All felled by Stoff

Maybe with a little help from me.

Or at least, that's how I decide to look at it.

EPILOGUE

The best time of year to catch trout in the stream at the edge of Segerstrom Ranch is autumn. Late autumn.

It's maybe five or six in the afternoon, and I've caught a baker's dozen already. Enough to do for dinner, but I'm still hoping for a couple more before sundown. I reach over to the cooler beside my chipped and weathered plastic lawn chair, fish another mystery beer out, pop the top and take a slug.

It's been years. Six long years without Stoff, but I still think about him every day. Hard not to, way things are. I see his legacy everywhere, in everything. I see it in the woods we ran through, see it in the hot curves of the road in summer, the way the snow gathers on the ground in winter. I hear his voice in the sharp, screaming calls of the mountain lions who stalk the hollow hills, and day by day, I hear it more and more in the voice of Cougar, our son.

Cougar. The first harling born among the Thuulhuum. None of us knew what to do when the egg that held him came – none of us had any medical experience, and none of us knew hara could even breed until I passed that stone. Weird fucking thing too, laying an egg. Hurt like hell, left me flat on my back for days. Egg was real ugly too, but something about it – I knew it was special. I knew it was something I had to protect, no matter how bizarre-looking it was.

A gift. That's how Stoff had put it. *A gift. Another lesson in what it means to be har.* I didn't understand it at the time of conception, didn't know what he meant, didn't think much of it until weeks after his death, when I could *feel* Cougar's egg growing in me. It *was* a gift, though, really. Having it, knowing what it was – it got me through one of the hardest periods in my life. It gave me the strength I needed to push on. I like to think it even carried me out of the darkness of the radio station where I lost him that day, that it was this gift of hope, this tiny mote of glowing life that brought me back to my feet. I doubt I ever would have crawled out of that darkness, doubt I ever would have found the strength to start again if it hadn't been for the spark of life he left me with.

A spark, yeah.

And a spark is all you need to start a fire.

The year that followed Stoff's death, I burned like a har on fire. It hurt like hell, being alone, my body going through all the weird changes that come with bringing a new life into this world. The hara of the hollow hills were all but gone – only a few of the Gold Country guys survived the machine massacre, and none of us really knew each other. Took weeks before we even began to speak to one another, much less start to assemble into any kind of coherent group.

And there was a lot of distrust in the beginning. There was a lot of fighting, vicious and violent. I saw a guy stabbed to death in the street in a disagreement over a can of food, joined with the mob that dragged his murderer off to the town hanging tree. Took a long time for us all to band together with any other kind of common purpose, but in the end, we managed to forge a sense of brotherhood that flickered and flared like a tiny flame on tinder. Winter came, cold and fierce – and that was all the push we needed to gather together the way we were always meant to, gather together not as disparate hara among the hollow hills, not as Uigenna, Varr or anything else, but as *Thuulhuum*. Gold Country folks, ghosts who haunt the ruins of the hollow hills, hunt side by side with the coyotes and the mountain lions.

As a tribe reborn, we claimed Segerstrom Ranch. We burned the bodies we found on the roads, in the fields, left the machines that crowded the streets of Cinder Hill to rust in the spring rains. Years passed, and with them, any sense of division or animosity. Cougar grew, and though he didn't have Stoff to help raise him, there was a whole village of fathers around looking out for his well being.

And he was the only kid among the Thuulhuum for a long time. Wasn't until just last year that another couple managed to conceive, but with people settling down more and more, I wouldn't be surprised if more will be on their way soon. It isn't easy, but we're discovering who we are, what we are. We're discovering what we can be, where we're going as a species. Maybe that's the real gift that Stoff gave us, gave me. Cougar's birth showed us what was possible, what we could achieve, and stories of Cinder Hill still fire the minds that hear them, urge all of us to reach out a little more each day, try something new, something harish instead of human.

"Dad," Cougar calls out, and I look back, smile at him. Five years old, give or take a few months, and he almost looks like a teenager already. These kids – these new kids, they grow fast. They're smart. They know things, know things they were never taught, least not by us.

"Yeah?"

"Gary and Irren said you might need help bringing dinner back."

I turn and glance at the sun, squint. Yeah, about that

time. When I turn back, I meet my son's eyes again, set the fishing pole in a cleft of rocks on the shore, gesture.

"Sure." I push myself up, stiff-legged in crusty jeans that by some miracle still fit me. Cougar is light on his feet, moves down the shallow rise with all the grace of the great cat he's named after. The fish I've caught are still swimming lazily in a pair of plastic five-gallon buckets that are more yellow than white after years of use. Cougar lifts one of the buckets by its shining steel handle, looks inside.

"Kinda small," he says, smiles.

"Small?" I grin back. "Only thing small around here is *you*, little squirt." I reach out, ruffle his hair even as he pulls away, laughing. Water sloshes in the bucket – I reach out, catch it by the rim, steady it, still grinning as I say, "don't drop our dinner, now."

"I won't." He smiles, and it's soft, innocent and sweet. A kid's smile. The smile of someone who hasn't known a different life from this. This world, all its weirdness – it's all normal to him, familiar, and I almost envy him for that. The ghosts of the world the way it once was are heavy on those of us who remember it, and the weight never seems to get much lighter, even with the passing of time.

"What else are they fixing up at the kitchen-house?" I ask him, hefting my own bucket.

"Salad again." He makes a face, unimpressed. I nod. Not surprising. Not much else to eat this time of year. The last of the peaches fell from the trees in the orchard weeks ago, and the first freezes have already killed off this year's tomato vines. Pumpkins and acorns – those are the two staple crops that'll be coming up next, ripe for harvest. Heavy breads, smoked fish and venison. That's what will get us through the coming winter.

We crest the rise of the gully where the creek runs, look down at the ranch that is our home. One of the guys is herding along the last of the chickens still hunting for bugs, pushing them toward the coop while a thin line of smoke rises from the chimney of the kitchen-house. In the pause, a goat grumbles around a mouthful of golden grass.

"Dad," Cougar says

"Yeah?"

"Tell me another story about papa." He looks up at me. "About my other dad."

I can't help but smile a little. "Okay."

And when I do, when words of the story start to weave themselves in the air, it doesn't hurt all that much.

For the first time in a long time, it actually makes me happy, hardly hurts at all.

GLOSSARY OF TERMS

Aghama, the – in Wraeththu lore, the first of all, the founder of their species, regarded among some hara as a god or demi-god.

Duwamish – previously the city of Seattle in America.

Har – a Wraeththu individual.

Harling – a young har, born of hara, not incepted, who is not yet at physical maturity.

Inception – the process by which a human becomes har, involving a transfusion of blood.

Kakkahaar – a Wraeththu tribe of the desert lands of Megalithica.

Manticker – also known as Manticker the Seventy, a famous har of the Uigenna tribe, (their phylarch, or leader, for some time), who once – allegedly – slew a troupe of seventy humans who attacked him, without taking injury himself.

Megalithica – the Wraeththu term for the Americas.

Thuulhuum – a Wraeththu tribe of The Rift of the Damned.

Uigenna – (Ew-ee-*gen*-ah) a tribe known to be the most savage among Wraeththu.

Unneah – (Oo-*nay*-uh) an offshoot of the Uigenna tribe who wished to establish a more peaceful way of living.

Varrs – a tribe of Wraeththu famed for their militaristic ways.

Wraeththu – (*Ray*-thoo) androgynous race that came to replace humanity.

ABOUT THE AUTHOR

 E.S. Wynn is the author of over fifty books in print. During the last decade, he has worked with hundreds of authors and edited thousands of manuscripts for nearly a dozen different magazines. His stories and articles have been published in dozens of journals, e-zines and anthologies. He has taught classes in literature, marketing, math, spirituality, energetic healing and guided meditation. Outside of writing, he has worked as a voice-over artist for several different horror and sci-fi podcasts, albums and ebooks. He has a bachelor's degree in English and is a proud Freemason.

E. S. Wynn's previous contributions to the Wraeththu Mythos are his short stories 'The Dehara of Navisalam' (*Para Imminence: Stories of the Future of Wraeththu* Immanion Press, 2012), 'Wolf', (*Para Kindred: Enigmas of Wraeththu*, Immanion Press, 2014) and 'Heart Howl' in the forthcoming *Para Animalia: Creatures of Wraeththu*, Immanion Press, (2015.)

Also From Immanion Press

Ghosteria: Volume One: The Stories by Tanith Lee
ISBN 978-1-907737-61-9 IP0118 £10.99, $19.99

In this new collection, which contains most of the ghost stories of Tanith Lee – including 4 new tales original to this volume – Lee slips freely through the full gamut of Fantasy, SF, Horror, Historical, Parallel and Contemporary genres. The themes range, amongst others, with a lost love in early 20th Century New Zealand, a bullied child in 1970's India, into the underhill palace of a brooding magician in search of wonders, among the guests of a modern spiky wedding-breakfast, and beside a psychic, on a far planet whose damson skies are adrift with flying whales...

The moods conjured are dark, unnerving or plain nasty; or else sad, tender, kind and - now and then – outright crazy. Turn up the light. And don't look behind you.

Ghosteria: Volume Two: The Novel: Zircons May be Mistaken by Tanith Lee
ISBN 978-1-907737-63-3 IP0119 £9.99, $18.99

Sometimes when people die, it comes as a great shock. Even to them...

A group of the dead linger here, in the yellow dwelling on the hill – once a castle, then a stately home, now falling into ruin.

These ghosts drift and mingle, and brood on their lost lives. Death can be caused by so many things – war, pandemics, ordinary murder – even suicide or accident. Even time. But after death, surely, one could hope for peace? Not any more.

For with 2020 the New Apocalypse began. Civilisation crashed, and outside this ancient building things terrible, predatory, mindless and unkillable roam and bellow.

Now all the lights have gone out for good –
Where do you turn?

The Moonshawl by Storm Constantine
ISBN: 978-1-907737-62-6 IP041 £11.99, $20.99

Ysbryd drwg… the bad ghost. Hired by Wyva, the phylarch of the Wyvachi tribe, Ysobi goes to Gwyllion to create a spiritual system based upon local folklore, but he soon discovers some of that folklore is out of bounds, taboo… Secrets lurk in the soil of Gwyllion, and the old house Meadow Mynd, home of the Wyvachi leaders. The house and the land are haunted. The fields are soaked in blood and echo with the cries of those who were slaughtered there, almost a century ago. Old hatreds and a thirst for vengeance have been awoken by the approaching coming of age of Wvya's son, Myvyen. If the harling is to survive, Ysobi must lay the ghosts to rest and scour the tainted soil of malice. But the ysbryd drwg is strong, built of a century of resentment and evil thoughts. Is it too powerful, even for a scholarly hienama with Ysobi's experience and skill? 'The Moonshawl' is a standalone supernatural story, set in the world of Storm Constantine's ground-breaking, science fantasy Wraeththu mythos.

Para Kindred, edited by Storm Constantine & Wendy Darling
ISBN: 978-1-907737-60-2 IP0040 £11.99 $20.99

The androgynous and mysterious Wraeththu have risen to replace humanity upon a ravaged world. Based on the world created by Storm Constantine, these stories explore different, intriguing aspects of bizarre mutations and specialisations that have arisen, hidden within the developing Wraeththu tribes and throughout the corners of the world. Shape-shifters, semi-mythological beings, or hara who have evolved in other unexpected ways, Para Kindred expands the horizons of the Wraeththu world. Para Kindred features two new stories each by Storm Constantine and Wendy Darling, plus contributions from Martina Bellovičová, Ash Corvida, Nerine Dorman, Suzanne Gabriel, Fiona Lane, Maria J Leel, Daniela Ritter and E S Wynn.

NewCon Press

http://newconpress.co.uk/

The very best in fantasy, science fiction, and horror

Colder Greyer Stones by **Tanith Lee**

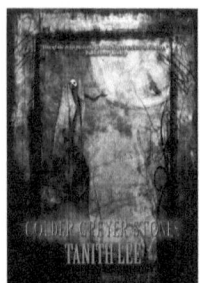

Released to commemorate the author being honoured with a Lifetime Achievement Award at the 2013 World Fantasy Convention, this stunning collection of stories provides further evidence of why Tanith Lee is held in such high regard by fans and contemporaries alike. The book features twelve wonderful, rich-textured tales including the brand new novelette "The Frost Watcher" and five stories previously available only in the (sold out) signed limited edition "Cold Grey Stones".

Paperback: ISBN 978-1-907069-60-4   £9.99

Pelquin's Comet (The Dark Angels, Book One) by **Ian Whates**

Action-packed space opera from the author of *The Noise Within*.

In an age of expansion, the crew of the freetrader Pelquin's Comet race to claim a cache of alien technology they hope will make them rich. Pursued by the authorities and by corporate agents, they battle against enemies without and within, all under the watchful eye of an unwelcome passenger: an agent of the bank funding their expedition, who is far more than he seems and may represent the deadliest threat of all.

Hardback ISBN: 978-1-907069-77-2   £25.99
Paperback ISBN: 978-1-907069-78-9   £12.99

www.ingramcontent.com/pod-product-compliance
Lightning Source LLC
Chambersburg PA
CBHW031231260626

47169CB00007B/2241